Good evening, Deputy Tucker. This isn't over. I want what you took from this house. I will get it back even if someone else gets hurt in the process.

Sydney stared at the cell-phone screen.

What was the sender talking about? She didn't take anything from this house. And how did he know she was here and would answer Dixon's phone?

Had he followed them? Was he outside now... watching?

"What's it say, Syd?" Russ crossed the space and dropped down next to her. He looked at the message and she heard him draw in a quick breath before jumping to his feet.

"Stay here," he commanded, and raced to the door. Gun in hand, he eased onto the porch, pulling the door closed behind him.

Wait. The text said if *someone* got hurt in the process. He didn't say if *she* got hurt. Did that mean he'd hurt people she cared about instead? Maybe even Russ?

She looked at the message again. But there it was right in front of her. His warning. This wasn't over and may not end before someone else died at the hands of this madman.

Books by Susan Sleeman

Love Inspired Suspense

High-Stakes Inheritance
Behind the Badge

SUSAN SLEEMAN

grew up in a small Wisconsin town where she spent her summers reading Nancy Drew and developing a love of mystery and suspense books. Today, she channels this enthusiasm into hosting the popular internet website *TheSuspenseZone.com* and writing romantic suspense and mystery novels.

Much to her husband's chagrin, Susan loves to look at everyday situations and turn them into murder and mayhem scenarios for future novels. If you've met Susan, she has probably figured out a plausible way to kill you and get away with it.

Susan currently lives in Florida, but has had the pleasure of living in nine states. Her husband is a church music director and they have two beautiful daughters, a very special son-in-law and an adorable grandson. To learn more about Susan, please visit www.SusanSleeman.com.

BEHIND THE BADGE

Susan Sleeman

LoveInspired

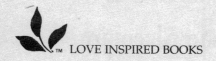 LOVE INSPIRED BOOKS

Recycling programs
for this product may
not exist in your area.

ISBN-13: 978-0-373-67468-8

BEHIND THE BADGE

Copyright © 2011 by Susan Sleeman

www.LoveInspiredBooks.com

Printed in U.S.A.

And we know that in all things
God works for the good of those who love Him,
who have been called according to His purpose.
—*Romans* 8:28

Dedication

For my husband, Mark, who always believes in me
and is by my side through good times and bad.
I couldn't do any of this without you.

Acknowledgments

Heartfelt thanks to:

My daughters, Erin and Emma,
for their tremendous support. Thank you, Emma, for
giving of your time to help brainstorm plot changes
and thank you, Erin, for the graphic-design expertise
that is at the heart of my promotional efforts.

My patient, sweet and talented editor, Tina James.
Thank you for continuing to have faith
in my stories. I am thrilled to be working with
and learning from you.

The very generous Ron Norris—
retired police officer with the LaVerne Police
Department—who gives of his time and knowledge
in both police procedures, as well as weapons
information. Ron, you are amazing! Any errors
in or liberties taken with the technical details
Ron so patiently explained to me are all my doing.

Sandra Robbins,
who always has a smile in her voice
and encouragement in her heart.
Thanks for being my supporter at all times.
God has blessed me with your friendship.

And most importantly, thank You, God,
for my faith and for giving me daily challenges
to grow closer to You.

ONE

Gunshots split the inky darkness.

Deputy Sydney Tucker hit the cold ground, a jagged rock slashing into her forehead on the way down. She reached for her service weapon. Came up empty-handed. She'd stopped after work to check on the construction of her town house and left her gun and cell phone in the car.

Dumb, Sydney. Really dumb. Now what're you gonna do?

Inching her head above knee-high grass, she listened. The keening whistle of the wind died, leaving the air damp and heavy with tension. Silence reigned.

Had she overreacted? Could be nighttime target practice. Hunters did crazy things sometimes.

Footfalls pounded from below. It sounded like two people charging through the brush. Maybe a chase. Then she heard a loud crash and branches snapping.

"What're you doin', man?" A panicked male voice

traveled through the night. "No! Don't shoot! We can work this out."

Three more gunshots rang out. A moan drifted up the hill.

Not target practice. Someone had been shot.

Sydney lurched to her feet, dizziness swirling through her. Blood dripped into her eyes. She wiped it away, blinked hard and steadied herself on a large rock while peering into the wall of darkness for the best escape route.

Heavy footfalls crunched up the gravel path.

"I know you're here, Deputy Tucker," a male voice, disguised with a high, nasal pitch, called out. "We need to talk about this. C'mon out."

Yeah, right. Come out and die. Not hardly.

Praying, pleading for safety, she scrambled deeper into the scrub. Over rocks. Through grass tangling her feet. Her heart pounded in her head, drowning the prayers with fear.

"I'm losing patience, Deputy," he called again in that strange voice. "You're not like Dixon. He had it coming. You don't."

Dixon? Did he mean the man she'd arrested for providing alcohol to her teenage sister and for selling drugs? Was that what this was about?

Rocks skittered down the incline. The shooter was on the move again. No time to think. She had to go. Now!

Blindly she felt her way past shrubs, over uneven ground. Dried leaves crunched underfoot. Branches slapped her face and clawed at her arms, but she stifled her cries of pain.

"I hear you, Deputy."

She wrenched around to determine his location. A protruding rock caught her foot, catapulting her forward. She somersaulted through the air. Her knee slammed into the packed earth and she crashed down the hill. Wrapping her arms around her head for protection, she tumbled and then came to a stop, breath knocked out of her, lying flat on her back in a thick stand of weeds.

"So you want to play it that way, do you, Deputy? Fine. Just remember, you can run, but you can't hide. I will find you. This will be resolved, one way or another." His disembodied laugh swirled into the night.

The darkness pressed closer. Blinding. Overwhelming. Terrifying.

She rose to her knees, but pain knifed into her knee, keeping her anchored to the ground.

Lord, please don't let me die like this. Give me the strength to move. I need to live for Nikki. She's only seventeen. She has no one.

Sydney uncurled and came to a standing position. Taking a few halting steps, she tested the pain. Nearly unbearable. But she *had* to do this for her sister.

Thinking of Nikki, she gritted her teeth and set off, moving slowly, taking care not to make a sound.

Out of the darkness, a hand shot out. Clamped over her mouth.

Screams tore from her throat, but died behind fingers pressed hard against her lips.

A muscled arm jerked her against a solid chest and dragged her deep into the brush.

God, please, no.

She twisted, arched her back, pushing against arms that held her like iron bands.

She dug her heels into the ground, but he was too strong. He kept going deeper into the brush before settling them both on the ground behind a large boulder.

"Relax, Sydney, it's Russ Morgan," her assailant whispered, his lips close to her ear.

Russ Morgan? What was Logan Lake's police chief doing here?

"Sorry to grab you." His tone said she was nothing more than a stranger instead of someone he'd known for years. "I didn't want you to alert the shooter with a scream. I'm gonna remove my hand now. Nod if you understand me."

She let all of her relief escape in a sharp jerk of her head. His fingers dropped away.

"Once the shooter rounded that curve, you would've been a goner," he whispered while still holding her firmly. "Good thing a neighbor reported gunshots."

Sydney started to shiver and inhaled deeply to steady her galloping pulse. Air rushed into her lungs. She was alive, but barely. No thanks to her own skills.

"You okay?" he asked, his breath stirring her hair.

"Yes." She willed her body to stop shaking and eased out a hiss of disappointment at her job performance. "How long have you been here?"

"Long enough to hear the shooter claim he's hit Dixon and is coming after you next," he whispered again, but urgency lit his voice and rekindled her fear. "This have to do with your arrest of Carl Dixon the other day?"

"I don't know," she whispered back. "I just stopped to check on the construction of my town house on my way home from work."

"Off duty, huh? Explains why you don't have your weapon drawn."

"I left my duty belt in my car." She waited for his reaction to not carrying, but he simply gave a quick nod as footfalls grated against gravel.

"Shh, he's about to pass us." Russ leaned forward and drew his gun with his free hand, but didn't release his hold on her.

Crunching steps came within a few feet of their location. Halted.

"Can you feel me breathing down your neck, Deputy? I'm inches from finding you." He didn't know the accuracy of his words.

She felt Russ pull in a deep breath, upping her concern and washing away the brief blanket of security his arms provided. Adrenaline urged her to move. To keep from panicking, she focused on Russ's unwavering weapon.

The shooter took a few steps closer. Her heart thumped, threatening to leave her chest. Russ tightened his hold as if he knew she wanted to bolt.

The shooter spun, sending gravel flying, then headed up the path.

As his footsteps receded, she tried to relax taut muscles. The warmth from Russ's body helped chase out her fear and the chill of the night. Thank God Russ was here. Who knows what would've happened if he hadn't come....

She refused to go there. God had watched over her. Provided rescue, just not in the form she'd have chosen.

Not only was Russ the head of the city's police force—a team often in competition with the county sheriff's department, where she worked—but he was a man she'd had a crazy crush on in high school. A man whose rugged good looks still turned women's heads.

She let out a long sigh.

"I know this is awkward," he whispered, "but hang tight for a few more minutes. We need to wait for him to head back down the hill."

She wanted to protest and suggest they flee now, but Russ thought clearly. Taking off now gave the killer the advantage of higher ground, making them moving targets. They'd have to sit like this until he passed them again.

If they made it out of here, which the approaching footfalls told her wasn't at all certain.

The shooter's steps pounded closer. He moved at a quick clip this time, as if he thought she'd gotten away and he was in hot pursuit. Or maybe he was heading to her car to lie in wait for her.

As the footsteps receded again, she felt Russ's arm slacken.

"Time to roll," he whispered. "Stay here."

"But I—"

"You have a backup?" He meant a backup gun that most officers carry on the job.

She shook her head.

"Then wait here." He gave her the hard stare that'd made him famous around town, and crept toward the path.

She leaned against the boulder and wrapped her arms around the warm circle on her waist where he'd held her. Without his warmth, she couldn't quit shaking. The reality of the night froze her inner core.

She should listen to Russ. Lie low. Wait until he apprehended the killer.

That was the safe thing to do.

The easy thing to do.

The wrong thing to do.

As an officer of the law, letting a shooter escape without trying to stop him wasn't an option. Even if that shooter had her in his sights, she'd make her way to her car for her gun and help Russ stop this maniac before he hurt anyone else.

* * *

Near the ditch, Russ came to a stop and fought to catch his breath. The taillights of a mud-splattered dirt bike vanished up the trail. He'd warned the suspect to stop, but short of shooting him in the back, Russ couldn't stop him from fleeing into the dark.

At least he'd accomplished his primary objective—to protect Sydney and keep her alive. Now he needed to alert his men and the sheriff's office to the suspect's whereabouts.

He lifted his shoulder mic and ordered a unit from his office to stake out the end of the trail for the motorcycle and to send an ambulance in case Dixon survived. Then he asked dispatch to patch him through to the county sheriff's department to make sure they knew he'd taken charge of the scene so none of their hotshot deputies arrived with the hope of usurping control.

He turned on his Maglite and headed up the hill. The beam of light skipped over gravel and lush plants lining the winding path. Midway up, rustling brush stopped him cold. He'd left Sydney higher up. Nearer the lake.

Was a second shooter hoping to ambush him?

He flipped off his light and sought protection behind a tree. His breath came in little pulses in the cold air—unusual for fall in Oregon. Adrenaline, with little time to ebb away, came roaring back, but even as the noise grew louder, he resisted the urge to take action.

Maybe it was Sydney. The girl he used to know wouldn't have listened to his directive and stayed put. She'd trounce down the hill, her chin tilted at the same insolent angle as when he told her he didn't return her crazy crush her freshman year of high school. Not that he'd wanted to send a beautiful, lively girl like her away. He could easily have dated her, but he was four years older, in college. With their age difference, it wouldn't have been right.

Bushes at the path's edge shook, then parted. Slowly, like a sleek panther, Sydney slipped out. He watched until she stood tall on those incredibly long legs he'd admired since she was sixteen before lowering his gun and aiming his flashlight at her.

She jumped and then peered up at him, an impudent look on her face. This was the Sydney he'd known as a teen and, heaven help him, in just minutes, she'd sparked his interest again.

"Care to shine that somewhere other than my face?" She shaded her eyes, warding off the glare.

He moved the light, but not before he caught a good look at a gaping wound running from her hairline to her eyebrow, covered in congealed blood. He lifted his hand to check out her injury, but stopped. He wouldn't probe a wound on one of his men's faces. As a fellow LEO—law enforcement officer—he wouldn't treat Sydney any differently.

"I told you to stay put." He infused his words with authority.

"I wanted to help." She held out blood-covered

hands. "Wish I'd listened… I tripped over the body." Her eyes watered as if she might cry.

Man…don't do that. Don't fall apart. He couldn't remain detached if she started crying. He'd have to empathize, maybe give her a reassuring pat on the arm. Maybe feel her pain and resurrect all the reasons he'd left his homicide job in Portland.

Changing his focus, he nodded at the brush. "Show me the body."

As the faint whine of sirens spiraled in the distance, she limped into tall grass, a grimace of pain marring her beautiful face. He followed, illuminating the area ahead of her. About ten feet in, she stopped suddenly.

Diffused rays slid over a young male lying on his back. Russ swung the beam to the man's face, landing on open eyes staring into the blackness above.

Sydney gasped and swung around him. She rushed toward the main path. Even though Russ knew it was a lost cause, he bent down to check for a pulse. As he suspected, this man hadn't made it and he ID'd him right away. Carl Dixon, a man every officer in the area knew from his frequent blips on the police radar, including his most recent arrest, for selling drugs.

All that ended with three gunshots to the chest at close range, from what Russ could see with his flashlight. Once they thoroughly processed the scene, he'd know more. But first, they needed to vacate the area before further contaminating the scene.

He found Sydney near the path, gaze fixed in the distance, hands clasped on her hips, exhaling long breaths as if trying to expel what she'd just seen.

Haunted eyes peered at him. "He's dead, right?"

"Yeah."

"And what about the killer?"

"Couldn't catch him. He took off on a dirt bike."

Disappointment crowded out the fear on her face. "Did you at least see him?"

"From the back. He was my height or a little taller, but lean. Wore a black stocking cap. The bike has a plate so it must be street legal. I caught the first few digits."

"That's something, then."

Russ didn't want to tell her it would do little for them in terms of searching DMV records, as three digits would return thousands of bikes, but he didn't think she could take any more bad news so he kept quiet. "Let's head down to the parking lot."

He gave her the flashlight and urged her to take the lead down the steep hill. Once on solid concrete, she handed it back to him. Holding it overhead, he watched her closely for dizziness or other impairments from her fall. He saw nothing out of the ordinary, but a head injury could mean a concussion. He'd have the EMTs check her out when they got there.

He pointed at a rough-hewn bench. "Maybe you should sit down."

"I'm fine." Her voice cracked and she seemed embarrassed about overreacting to the murder.

"It's okay to be upset, Syd. A horrible thing happened tonight."

"I'm fine, really. I'll be back to a hundred percent by morning."

"Don't expect too much too fast."

"I said I'm fine." She straightened her shoulders into a hard line. "It may be my first year on the job, but I can handle this."

"You just witnessed a homicide. If you're like other officers, you're probably feeling guilty for not preventing it."

"I deserve the blame," she said, her eyes overflowing with guilt. "I should've been carrying. Now a person is dead and a killer is running free. What if he hurts someone else?"

Russ knew that look. Had worn it himself. He took a step closer and softened his voice. "You can't think that way, Syd. You have a life outside the job. You couldn't have known something like this would happen when you left your gun in the car."

She backed away, studied his face for long moments, her pained expression turning suspicious. "What's going on here? Is this about me being a woman?" She pulled her shoulders even higher.

"What?"

"If I was a guy, you'd be jumping down my throat

and railing on me for being dumb enough not to carry at all times." Her voice had turned angry.

He held up his hands and took a moment to re-group.

Maybe she was right. Not in the way she meant, discriminating against her because he thought a woman couldn't do this job. This had more to do with their past. He'd never interacted with Sydney the deputy, just Sydney, the woman with captivating blue eyes that could leave a man thinking about her into the wee hours of the night.

He needed to adjust his thinking and see the fiercely determined deputy standing before him. She was trying so hard to overcome her guilt and hold herself together at a time when many rookies fell apart.

He'd respect that and get on with it. "All I'm trying to say is I've been where you are, and I'm here if you want to talk about it. But we can move on." He paused, waited until her anger receded a bit. "How about telling me what happened before I got here?"

She shielded her eyes from the light. "There's really nothing much to add. I was on the hill check-ing on the construction of my town house. I heard gunshots and dived for cover. The killer called out my name, asking me to come out." She shivered, then clamped a hand on the back of her neck as if she could stop it. "He said he wanted to talk to me, but I think that was just his way of luring me out so he could kill me, too."

"You made so much noise falling down that hill, he had to know your location. If he wanted to take you out, even with your vest on, a few rounds in your direction would've done it."

"So you think he really *did* want to talk to me about something. But what?"

"We figure that out, we ID our killer. The first step is analyzing your connection to Dixon."

"No real connection. I arrested him a few times, but that's all. I—" Her voice drifted off as flashing lights rounded the bend in the road, catching her attention.

His men were almost here. He wanted to keep questioning her, but she was distracted. He needed to move her out of the action.

"I need to get Officer Garber to secure the area. You can wait in your car and we'll continue this when I'm done."

She opened her mouth as if to question his decision, but then closed it. He escorted her to the car and watched as she gingerly settled in, a soft moan escaping when she bent her knee.

"I need to call this in to my supervisor." She picked up her cell from the cup holder.

Great. Krueger.

Sergeant Karl—with a *K*—Krueger, as he liked to call himself, had also applied for the chief's job, and when the council selected Russ over him, a fierce rivalry developed. If Krueger, representing the county sheriff's department, showed up and offered to help in the investigation, and Russ turned him away, Krueger would let it slip to the public that the city police—and Russ—weren't doing all they could to catch this killer.

Maybe he could convince Sydney to hold off. "Do you really want Krueger coming out here right now?"

"Honestly, no. Fortunately, he's out of town until tomorrow, but I still need to call in."

Yes, finally, something in his favor tonight.

"Go ahead, then. I'll be right back." Russ crossed the lot to meet Bill Garber, his most senior officer.

He'd climbed from his car and was surveying the area. Russ could see the excitement of a murder investigation burning in Garber's eyes. Not that Garber would be happy someone died, but the thrill of using skills he didn't normally get to use in this small town was intoxicating.

Russ met him at the road. "I want this entrance sealed off. No traffic, foot or vehicle, beyond that bench." He pointed at the bench near the path. "And call the ME. Tell him to hurry. With the fog moving in we need to get the body out of here before we can't see anything."

Garber nodded. "Should I call county for their portable lights in case?"

That's what Russ liked about Garber. Always one

step ahead. "Do that. Let me know what they say. I'll be at Deputy Tucker's cruiser taking her statement."

Garber's eyes filled with questions, but Russ walked away. He wouldn't waste time now bringing Garber up to speed. Back at Sydney's car, Russ chose not to sit but stood next to the door. That way he could block her view of the scene and keep an eye on what was going on at the same time.

He focused on Sydney for the moment. "So tell me about Dixon's arrests."

She swiveled to face him. "The first time was last month when I busted a party at his house and hauled him in for supplying alcohol to minors."

"Your sister, Nikki, was involved, right?"

She nodded. "Dixon got her and three of her friends stinking drunk and the judge let him off with a fine. A *fine*. Can you imagine that?" Her voice rose with each word. "He corrupts young girls, pays a few bucks and is free to do it again."

"Sometimes our system doesn't work."

"Yeah, well, try to act so complacent when it happens to someone you love."

She had a good point. How would he react if this happened to his seven-year-old son, Zack? Not that Russ would find himself in this position. He'd let alcohol control his life for a few years and now only had weekend visits with his son. They spent every waking moment together so this couldn't happen.

But as a father, Russ could still understand why Sydney reacted this way.

"I'm sure I wouldn't let it roll off my back real easy."

"And I couldn't either. She's my little sister, Russ. I fed her. Changed her diapers. Loved her when both our parents failed us." She paused. Breathed deeply. "I couldn't let Dixon get away with hurting her and walking free. He had to pay."

"You wanted him dead," he added, to see her reaction.

"What? No! Of course not. I just wanted him in jail. I knew he'd screw up again so I made it a point to follow him in my free time." She met his eyes. "Last Wednesday afternoon I caught him on his porch selling coke and busted him."

He couldn't believe it. She'd gone rogue and followed the guy, putting herself in danger. "They call it *off duty* for a reason, Syd. Without backup, you could get into serious trouble. Besides, you don't have the experience to run a narcotics investigation."

"Believe me, I'm well aware of my limitations. When I started following him, I didn't know it would lead to drugs. Or to this." She held out her bloody hands. "If I'd known my actions would result in someone's death, I would never have pursued him." She shivered and wrapped her arms around her waist, sheer misery clouding her face.

He hated to see any officer forced to deal with

death, and he hadn't wanted to make things worse. Still, he had a job to do. That meant tough discussions like this would occur. But he could try to make it easier.

He went to his trunk, grabbed a blanket and settled it over her shoulders. Raw anguish filled her eyes.

Russ felt her pain.

To the bone.

He had lived it for the past four years, since he'd watched a homicide suspect gun down a six-year-old boy. Watched, helplessly, in slow motion.

Russ wanted to go back. Save Willie Babcock's life. But that wasn't possible. The price had been paid. Willie with his life. Russ with the loss of his family.

He shook off the emotions, dug deep for the calm center he'd worked so hard to develop the past few years. He couldn't change the past, but he could stop it from happening again.

He'd do everything within his power to find the killer so another person didn't die on his watch.

TWO

Heavy banks of fog drifted off the lake and rolled across the cement, as if alive and breathing. Damp and irritated from the mist, Russ stood in the parking lot next to Garber, waiting for him to conclude his call with the sheriff's department.

On a good day, waiting around got on Russ's nerves, but tonight it left him with too much time to think about Sydney's wounded expression. Something that was definitely not in his best interest.

Garber clapped his phone closed and turned to Russ. "Not good news. This fog has the sheriff's department swamped. They're investigating a hit-and-run on the south side of the county and using their only set of lights. We won't get them until they finish."

"Any idea of time?"

"Could be a few hours or not at all if they have another problem," Garber replied.

"No sense in all of us standing around. Call Dixon's landlord back. Tell him I'm on my way to the house and to meet me there. Call me when the lights arrive or if anything else develops."

Heading in Sydney's direction, he saw her sitting on the bumper of a silent ambulance, its red light swirling through the fog in an eerie dance. She'd washed the blood from her hands and pulled her hair into a ponytail, which emphasized the angry gash on her head, now swollen to a massive purple lump. At least the bleeding had subsided, thanks to EMT Lisa Watson, who'd applied a neat row of butterfly bandages.

"That'll do for now." Lisa pressed her finger on the bottom bandage.

Sydney winced, then forced a laugh. "Will I live?"

"Looks worse than it is. I closed the wound, but it could still scar. You might want to have a doctor take a look at it."

"Or not. But thanks, Lisa." Sydney smiled up at Lisa, a genuine, warm smile like the one she'd radiated up at Russ as a teen, almost overpowering his common sense in sending her away.

He shook off the thought. He was here to do a job. Catch a killer. Not let the cute dimples or generous smattering of freckles dotted across high cheekbones distract him.

He stepped into his professional mode and approached the pair. "So Deputy Tucker's good to go, then?"

Lisa nodded. "She'll be fine with some rest and over-the-counter pain relievers."

"Then if you'll excuse us, I need to have a word with her."

"I'll be taking off," Lisa said to Sydney. "I'm off duty in an hour or so, but you can call me any time tonight if you need something."

"Thanks again, Lisa." Sydney shoved off the bumper, grimacing on the way up.

He nodded at the jagged slit in her pant leg, darkened with blood. "Looks like your forehead isn't your worst problem."

"I'll ice my knee when I get home. It'll be fine." She turned her gaze to the officers at the base of the path. "Any leads?"

"That's what I wanted to talk to you about. We're waiting on your department to deliver lights, so I'm heading over to Dixon's place and wanted you to accompany me."

"Me?" Her eyes widened.

He laughed. "Don't sound so surprised."

"You have to admit it's not common practice to ask for a rookie's help."

"Normally I wouldn't, especially when you're the closest thing we have to a witness on this case, but I'm hoping a trip to Dixon's house will jog your memory and give us a lead." Before she could ask another question, he held his hand toward the road. "My cruiser's over there."

Though her gaze still held questions, she started

toward his car. He heard her groan in pain, but kept his mouth shut. The less he said about her injuries, the less likely he would make a comment that she misunderstood. For the same reason, he didn't open the passenger door for her as he would in a social situation, just climbed behind the wheel. When she settled into the other seat, he eased onto the road.

Pulling out her seat belt, she suddenly let it go. "My gun. It's still in my car."

"Relax. You won't need it at Dixon's house."

Sighing, she retrieved the belt. "You must think I'm hopeless at this job."

He could hear the despondency and self-recrimination in her voice. She had to find a way to deal with the guilt. Not the way he had, with a stiff drink, but by talking and working through it.

He gave her what he hoped was a comforting smile. "Good officers aren't born, Syd. They learn through experience."

"But you'd never leave your gun in the car."

"No, you're right. But I might've as a rookie. All you can do is learn from tonight and adjust accordingly." Trying not to feel so much like a hypocrite by telling her one thing and still letting Willie's death get to him, he eased through light traffic.

"Not that this is an excuse." She shifted to face him. "But I like to do something positive on my way home to help relieve the stresses of the day. Part of that is leaving my duty belt behind. It's like taking off the weight of the belt helps remove the weight of the job."

He didn't know what to say that he hadn't already said, other than telling her about Willie. And for the first time in years, he wanted to tell someone.

He opened his mouth, but the words didn't come. Other than his partner, he'd never talked with another LEO about Willie. They'd have told him to let it go. That he wasn't at fault. A second search wasn't protocol. But Russ learned early in the job to take extra precautions. He just didn't follow his instincts that particular day. And it still haunted him.

So much so he still couldn't talk about it, so he focused on his driving, taking the shortest route to Dixon's house. Making the final turn, he caught sight of Sydney's questioning gaze.

"What?" he asked, hoping she hadn't been watching him battle warring emotions.

"What do *you* do to let go of a bad day?"

He shrugged. "My biggest problems are often bureaucracy or the budget. Not finding a killer."

"So what about tonight? When you get home, how are you gonna let this go?"

"I haven't had to deal with real stress since leaving Portland, so I don't really know." And he hadn't had to deal with it since he put his drinking days behind him. So what *would* he do tonight?

"So why'd you leave, anyway?"

Searching for the right address, he slowed. "You're full of questions."

"I'm just trying to learn how to handle the job, Russ. It's different from what I thought it would be. Especially tonight." She rubbed a hand over her eyes. "I know we're told to expect to see people die in car crashes, but I honestly never thought I'd see someone gunned down."

This experience could make her walk away from the job. A job she excelled at, from what he'd heard through the grapevine. She was known for being patient. Understanding. Intuitive. Sure, she'd panicked tonight, but law enforcement would lose out if a rookie with her promise quit. Hopefully, he could help restore her confidence during the investigation.

He tipped his head out the window. "That Dixon's house, with the big porch?"

"Yeah, that's it." She peered out the window. "I can't see how this visit will help. Nothing much happened here. It was a simple drug bust."

"Try to let go of that notion or you might block anything that could help us." He slid into a parking space.

He climbed out and a feeling of unease settled over him.

The wind howled through trees, whipping the fine mist into his face. He looked at Dixon's house. Surveyed the ragged shrubs. The dark porch. Saw nothing out of the ordinary. Searched the street, peering into the deep shadows running the length of the house.

"What is it?" Sydney asked coming up behind him and startling him.

"Nothing."

She narrowed her eyes. "Then why are you so jumpy?"

"I have the feeling our suspect is watching us."

He saw a fresh wave of fear grip her face and instantly wanted to take back his words. But maybe scaring her a bit wasn't a bad thing. If it didn't paralyze her like earlier tonight, and made her more vigilant, a little fear was just what she needed to stay one step ahead of their killer.

Russ's concern upping hers, Sydney looked across the street at the small white bungalow illuminated under a streetlight. The fog swirling around the lake hadn't arrived in town. She could clearly see white paint rising in papery peels on old clapboard siding. The stirring breeze moved overgrown grass and carried the flakes into the air, depositing them like snow on the unkempt yard.

A yard that was as overgrown as when she'd arrested Dixon three days ago.

Only three days.

Seemed like a lifetime ago. Maybe in another world. A world before the roller coaster of emotions that raced through her heart tonight. Up. Down. Around. One minute she was fine. The next nearing panic and letting guilt threaten to swamp her with tears. But she wouldn't cry in front of Russ. Even if he seemed to understand what she was going through.

He nodded at the house. "Since Mr. Becker's not here with the key yet, we can run through Dixon's arrest. Where were you when you saw the deal go down?"

"Behind a big pine at the edge of those woods." She pointed across the street. "I had to work in a few hours and didn't want Dixon to see my cruiser, so I left it a few blocks away and walked over here."

"So then you had a clear view of the house. What time of day was it?"

"Around three."

"Good. Daylight. Easy to see something that at first glance didn't seem important. Take me through the arrest."

"When I arrived, I could tell a party was going on from the noise. About an hour later, Nikki's old friend Julia came walking down the street from the east. I knew she had a drug problem, so I figured she was here to get her next fix from Dixon." Sydney shook her head. "You should've seen her, Russ. She was such a mess. I hated to arrest her, but she wasn't the sweet kid I used to know anymore. She's in rehab right now. I sure hope it sticks."

"The arrest might be just what she needed to kick the addiction." He offered her a reassuring smile.

She hoped he was right, but her gut said Julia had a long road ahead of her.

"So what happened next?" he asked.

"Julia knocks on the door, and Dixon comes out. She exchanges cash for a baggie. I call it in to dispatch, then head across the street, slap the cuffs on Dixon and convince Julia not to run. Then we wait for backup and round up the partygoers for possession."

"So no one fled the scene?"

"Not really. There was a girl standing by a motorcycle a few cars down who walked away when I came up, but I'm not sure she was involved."

His face lit up. "A motorcycle? Can you describe it?"

"I can do better than that. While I was watching the house, I snapped a few pictures of the area. I know I got a shot of the bike."

"Maybe our killer knows about the pictures and there's something in them that could incriminate him." His tone rose with interest.

She dug out her cell and thumbed through the pictures. Russ moved behind her, and she felt his breath whisper over her neck, below her ponytail. She had to fight to concentrate on the images. He lifted her hand closer to his face. The warmth of his hand covering hers almost made her turn to see if the touch affected him, too. But he stabbed a finger at the current picture and she knew his focus remained on the case.

"That looks like the bike our suspect took off on tonight. Can't make out the plate, but if we enlarge it we might hit pay dirt." He let go of her hand. "Officer Garber is a motorcycle enthusiast. He might see something in this picture that we don't."

An older-model car with a rumbling muffler chugged down the street emitting waves of smoke and pulling up in front of the house.

"That's Mr. Becker," Russ said. "Time to check out the house."

Russ greeted the older man whose face held enormous respect for Russ. Locals appreciated his experience, diplomacy and the way he kept the department operating so efficiently.

Thinking about what she'd heard around town about Russ, Sydney watched as he talked with Mr. Becker.

Everyone in town knew Russ was divorced with a young son who spent occasional weekends with him. Especially the single women who thought they could crack his hard shell and win the man who seemed to need no one. But other than that, no other rumors had spread about the ten or so years he'd been gone from Logan Lake. She hadn't really wondered about him, but tonight she wished she knew a little more about him.

Shaking Mr. Becker's hand through the open window, Russ caught her watching him. She wanted to look away, but his gaze met hers. He'd only smirk if she suddenly averted her eyes. So she kept them firmly fixed to his and was surprised when he responded by staring deeply into her eyes as if searching for something.

But as Mr. Becker handed Russ the key, he broke eye contact. He promised to lock up and return the key, then waited for Mr. Becker to drive off before heading her way.

Wondering what that look had been about, she waited for him to pass and climbed the stairs behind him. On the porch, memories from the arrest floated up, replacing her thoughts of Russ.

With gloved hands, he turned the key in the lock. She accompanied him into the house. As she looked around, she snapped on gloves.

"Look the same as when you arrested him?" Russ asked.

"Minus the beer cans and rowdy friends, yes."

"You arrest these friends?"

"Yeah, we found lines of coke on the table, so we hauled them all in."

He crossed to the desk, drew open a drawer. "We'll need to question them. I'll want a copy of your arrest report first thing in the morning."

Sydney nodded, though it would have to be second thing in the morning. Her sergeant would want to blast her first for leaving her gun in the car.

She saw a cord trailing from an outlet and found a charger holding a phone hidden under a table. "Odd place to charge a phone," she said, dropping down to her knees.

"We didn't find a cell on the body so I was hoping

it'd be here." Russ's tone was the most optimistic she'd heard all night. He tossed her a plastic evidence bag. "Bag it."

She settled the phone into the bag. As she laid it on the table, it chimed a text.

"There's no way I'm ignoring that." Through the bag, she fiddled with buttons until it unlocked. "It's from someone Dixon has labeled as Boss."

"Read it to me."

She opened the message.

Good evening, Deputy Tucker. This isn't over. I want what you took from this house. I will get it back even if someone else gets hurt in the process.

Her mouth fell open, and she stared at the screen.

What was he talking about? She didn't take anything from this house.

And how did he know she was here and would answer Dixon's phone?

Had he followed them? Was he outside now... watching?

"What's it say, Syd?"

She heard Russ's voice but couldn't quit staring at the screen or form the words to tell him about the message. Their theory had been right. The killer did want something from her.

But what, she had no clue. She felt powerless.

Russ crossed the space and dropped down next to her.

"Let me see." His voice was soft, reassuring, but didn't melt the ice forming around her heart.

He tried to take the phone. Her fingers clamped around it like a vise. She couldn't seem to let go. He turned her hand. She heard him draw in a quick breath before jumping to his feet.

"Stay here," he commanded and raced to the door. Gun in hand, he eased onto the porch, pulling the door closed behind him.

He needn't have told her to stay put. Without her gun, she wasn't moving a muscle. Especially not to go outside. The killer was likely hanging in the shadows of the trees. A mere shadow himself. Watching through the misty rain. Biding his time. Hoping to strike again.

Wait. The text said if *someone* got hurt in the process. He didn't say if *she* got hurt. Did that mean he'd hurt people she cared about instead? Maybe even Russ?

She dropped the phone and flew to the window. Searched up and down the street. Not seeing Russ, she opened the door. Poked her head out. She heard footfalls at the side of the house.

Was it Russ or the killer? Should she stay out here or go inside?

She scanned the area, her mind churning with indecision. The footfalls grew closer. She slipped back inside the doorway but kept the door open a crack. A hand holding a gun cleared the side of the house. She glimpsed a deep navy sleeve covering the arm. Russ?

She held her breath. Waited.

Russ emerged from the shadows, his profile strong and solid. She whooshed out the breath. Dragged a fresh one into her lungs.

He spun and fixed his gun on her. He hissed out a breath. "Go inside and close the door, Syd."

Sirens split the air. Red lights twirled in the distance, coming closer. Knowing backup was moments away and their killer wouldn't try anything with several officers on the scene, she took cover in the house.

"Lord, please protect Russ," she cried out, and settled on the floor with the phone.

Hoping it was a bad dream, she looked at the message again. But there it was right in front of her. His warning. That this wasn't over and might not end before someone else died at the hands of a madman.

THREE

After Russ and his men searched fruitlessly for the killer, he went back inside the house. He found Sydney sitting on the floor, Dixon's phone still in hand. He squatted next to her and took the phone, still in its evidence bag.

"We'll get him before he hurts anyone else, Syd. I promise." He didn't know how he could say that. He could no more promise this guy wouldn't hurt anyone than he could promise she'd be fine.

"Promise me something else."

"What?" he asked gruffly.

"That you'll let me work on the investigation with you."

"I—"

She held up her hands. "Don't say no right away. Just think about it. I may be a rookie, but I also seem to hold the key to this case. I didn't take anything from this house, but our killer thinks I did and he seems more than willing to come after me to get it."

He let himself spend a few moments peering into her eyes, thinking how much she'd changed and yet how much she hadn't. Her eyes seemed bluer, her face softer. If he didn't move away from the pull of her gaze, he'd promise her the moon.

He stood. "All I can say right now is I'll think about it."

"Fair enough."

The door opened and Officer Baker came into the house. Russ went to meet him.

"Here's the phone." Russ handed the bag to Baker, who was busy checking out Sydney.

Russ got in his face. "I want a log of every call and number on here before you go home for the night. And put some pressure on the phone company to get Dixon's past phone logs ASAP. Call me as soon as the log is finished."

"You got it," Baker said, his eyes returning to Sydney.

"Let's step outside, Baker." Russ bit back his irritation and went out. "What's wrong with you? Staring at Deputy Tucker like that. She's a capable officer just like us and deserves respect."

"Sorry, Chief. I didn't mean anything by it. As you say she's a capable officer, but—don't jump down my throat for this—you have to admit she's nothing like us." He grinned.

Russ would admit no such thing aloud and definitely not to one of his officers. "Get out of here and get to work on the phone."

Russ couldn't blame Baker for noticing Sydney. He'd done the same thing when his only thoughts should be about protecting her. He needed to keep his focus. Especially out here.

He made a quick sweep of the area. He'd left one unit stationed out front so they could finish searching Dixon's house without worrying about the killer.

Russ felt as if the creep was long gone, but he couldn't help worry about what his next move would be or if Russ would be with Sydney when he did strike again. Maybe Russ should call county and ask them to arrange protection for her.

No. Not a good idea.

If he went that route, Russ would have to deal with Krueger all the time just to talk to Sydney. He could ask to have her assigned to the investigation as she'd requested. She'd not only be available when needed, but he could also keep an eye on her to make sure she didn't come to any harm.

Yeah, that's what he'd do.

Before he changed his mind, he made a quick call to Lieutenant James, who was most obliging. Krueger would be miffed when he heard Russ went over his head, but Russ could handle it.

He made one last sweep of the area then went inside.

"Let's finish this place up and get out of here." He returned to the desk. "Oh, by the way. I called Lieutenant James while I was outside. He agreed to put you on the team. You'll report to me until this investigation is closed."

She smiled. "That's great, Russ. Thank you."

"You can thank me by being extra vigilant until this killer is caught." He let his gaze connect with hers. "Keep your head on a swivel. Wear your vest at all times." He wanted to add *Sleep in it, too,* but he knew that would only earn him a roll of her eyes.

"Don't worry, Russ. I hear you." She turned back to digging through the sofa. "Found some weed. Didn't take Dixon long after getting out to replenish his stock."

Russ sat on a chair and dug deeper into a bottom drawer. He pulled out a power cord from a computer. "Did you take a laptop into evidence?"

She shook her head. "We saw that power cord, but no computer."

"Maybe that's what our suspect thinks you took."

"Could be, I guess. Though I don't know what kind of evidence a drug dealer would have on a computer."

They worked for another hour, but didn't locate anything else of interest so Russ decided to call it quits. At the door, he said, "I still want to show those pictures of the motorcycle to Garber if you're up for it."

"Sure."

They stepped onto the porch, where the whispery mist had turned to soft rain. The temperature had dropped when the rain came in, and neither of them wore jackets.

Sydney shivered and nodded at the patrol car sitting at the curb. "What's he doing here?"

"Just a precaution."

"You thought the killer might come back." The worry returned to her eyes.

He scanned the area on the way to his cruiser, but tried not to be obvious about it and raise her concern even more. He nodded at his officer to let him know he could leave.

At the car, Russ opened the trunk, retrieved his jacket and draped it over Sydney's shoulders.

"You keep it," she said. "You're cold, too."

"I'm fine." He moved to open her door before remembering not to. Not saying anything, she tugged his jacket tightly around her shoulders and climbed in.

On the road, she didn't speak. He didn't mind the silence. He used the quiet to keep his focus on making sure the killer wasn't following. When they pulled up to the town houses, he was certain no one tailed them. Of course, that didn't mean their killer hadn't left Dixon's house and returned before them.

Feeling the killer's eyes on them, Russ shifted into Park and searched the area. Dense woods and heavy undergrowth made plenty of places to hide. The rain, growing thicker by the minute, gave him even more cover.

Russ turned to tell Sydney to wait here and he'd drive her home, but a car fishtailed to a stop across the road, drawing his interest. The passenger door opened, emitting throbbing music. A young teen climbed out.

"Nikki?" Sydney said on a whisper.

"What's your sister doing here?"

"I don't know, but don't worry. I'll make sure she leaves right away." She started to open the door but he grabbed her arm.

"You think that's such a good idea?" he asked.

"Her leaving a murder scene? Of course."

"What if our killer got here before us and is watching you? Even in this weather it's easy to see her resemblance and figure out she's your sister. He could see Nikki leave. Follow her to—"

"Get to me." Sydney finished his sentence.

"Exactly."

A plethora of emotions shifted over Sydney's face. Worry morphed into rage, the exact emotion he'd feel if Zack were targeted by a murderer. He would do anything to keep his son out of the hands of a killer. Russ could understand the thoughts traveling through Sydney's mind and knew she was probably thinking like a parent, not a deputy.

Resolve tightened her eyes. "I'll take her home with me."

"I'll drive you."

She arched a perfectly plucked eyebrow. "I don't need a babysitter, Russ."

"I know, but humor me. Once I show Garber those pictures, I won't be needed here until the lights arrive."

"That doesn't mean you need to escort me home."

"I think I do." He held up his hand before she argued more. "This event tonight has made you more of a victim than a deputy and you aren't at the top of your game. Worrying about your sister is just an added distraction. If the suspect follows you, it would be good to have another officer present."

She glanced across the lot in the direction of the other officers. "I can't see you telling one of your men to duck and cover like this."

"You're wrong. If one of my men were in this situation—" he paused, locking eyes with her to communicate the truth in his words "—I'd make sure he was escorted home. I would never do anything to endanger their lives. I'll do no less for you."

He was afraid he'd scared her again by the over-the-top intensity in his tone, but she simply shrugged. "Okay...but we take my car. I'll need it in the morning."

"Fine, but I'll drive."

She leaned closer and her eyes burned into him. "I don't like this, Russ. Not one bit. Your officers will think I'm soft and need coddling, but your points are valid. Nikki's safety comes before my reputation. If you think driving my car will accomplish that, then I'll agree."

"You made the right decision, Syd."

The roll of her eyes said she thought otherwise. "Here's my phone. I'll get Nikki and wait at my car." She handed it to him.

"I'll walk with you." He got out and came alongside her.

An uneasy feeling settled over him again. He searched the scrub lining the road. Nothing. So why did he keep feeling as if the killer was watching them, waiting for Russ to turn away to strike?

He glanced back at Sydney, vulnerable and scared for her sister. Now he had two people to protect from a killer.

Could he keep them safe or was he fooling himself?

A fresh wave of apprehension washed over him. Visions of Willie falling to the ground flashed into his mind.

Let it go, Russ.

He couldn't let the raw pain from Willie's death rise up and make him paranoid. Emotions like that only led to two things in his life. Mistakes and regret. He had to keep his head and apprehend this creep before he returned, got the information he wanted from Sydney and ended her life.

Sydney didn't know what to say to Nikki. Her training as a deputy didn't prepare her for this situation, and her role as Nikki's surrogate mom didn't, either. Only God could give her the right words, now.

Father, I need Your help. Everything is crumbling around me. People are getting hurt or this madman is threatening to hurt them and now I have to tell Nikki about him. Give me the words, Lord, and help me keep her safe.

She took Nikki's arm and moved her behind the protection of a van. "What're you doing here, Nikki?"

"We heard about the shooting on Mr. Clark's scanner." She shook off Sydney's hand. "You always stop here on the way home. When you didn't answer your phone, I got worried. So Emily brought me." Nikki pointed at her best friend, Emily Clark, who waved at them from the driver's seat of her car.

"It was sweet of you to check on me, Nikki, but I'm fine and this is no place for either of you to be."

"You don't look fine." Nikki stared at Sydney's forehead, then whistled. "That's some awful shade of purple already."

Sydney smiled her thanks for Nikki's concern. It had been a long time since her sister said anything nice to her. A month, to be exact. Since the drinking episode at Dixon's house, after which Sydney had grounded Nikki.

Hoping she'd learned her lesson, and hoping to repair the relationship that had been deteriorating of late, she'd agreed to let Nikki spend the night at

Emily's house. Now she had to tell Nikki that she needed to come home.

So what did she say without giving her the gory details of the murder and scaring her?

"I know that face, Syd." Nikki drew her attention. "What'd I do now?"

"You shouldn't be here. This is a crime scene and you need to leave."

"Yes, ma'am." Nikki saluted, but her tone didn't hold the usual sarcasm. "Is it all right if Emily and I stop for some ice cream on the way to her house?"

Sydney took a deep breath before breaking the bad news. "I really wish I could let you go with Emily, but you need to come home with me tonight."

"What?" Nikki cried, drawing stares from the officers. "This is a joke, right?"

"No joke. Something's come up."

Nikki pouted. "No, it didn't. You just figured if I left her house tonight that I'd do it again. Admit it. You don't trust me."

Her sullen tone hit Sydney like a punch to the gut. "That's not it."

"You just want to ruin my life."

Sydney hated to tell Nikki what was going on, but if she didn't her sister wouldn't understand. Their relationship would only suffer. "This wasn't just a case of gunshots being fired tonight. A man was murdered."

"What?"

"Someone killed Carl Dixon."

Nikki's mouth dropped open, and she brought a hand up to cover it.

Sydney moved closer and laid a hand on her sister's shoulder. "That's why I need you to come home."

"I'm really sorry he got killed, Syd, but what does it have to do with me? I only went to a party at his house—I didn't, like, know him or anything."

"This is about me, not you. Three days ago, I arrested him for selling drugs to Julia. Seems like whoever killed him thinks I took something from the house and he wants it back." She took a deep breath. "He tried to kill me tonight, too."

"No way."

"Unfortunately, yes. He could come after me again or even you."

"Me?" Nikki's tone squeaked higher. "Why me?"

"It's a long shot, but he could go after you to get to me. I want you with me so I can protect you. Until the killer is found, I'll need you to stay close to home."

"But what about Emily's birthday party? It's tomorrow night." She pleaded with Sydney. "You said I could go. Promised, even."

"I'm sorry, Nikki. I don't like to break a promise, but this's out of my control."

Nikki crossed her arms. "You're not sorry at all. Ever since you became a cop all you want to do is keep me locked up in the house."

"That's not true. What I want is to help you

become everything you can be in life. Sometimes that means being the bad guy."

"Whatever." Nikki's nostrils flared in anger.

"I want you to call Emily. Tell her you're coming home with me, but don't say anything about the murder."

"I'll just go over and tell her," she huffed.

"No—call her. I want you to stay behind the van. This guy could be hiding around here, and I won't risk exposing you."

Fear sparked in Nikki's eyes. Sydney hated that she was the cause of it, but sometimes you had to do the hard things to protect the ones you love. The text from the killer proved he'd stop at nothing to retrieve the item he was looking for, and she wasn't about to let this crazed man anywhere near her sister.

FOUR

After cleaning up in the bathroom, Russ sat in the tiny dining area in Sydney's duplex, pulling sandwiches from a bag. Since none of them had eaten, they'd grabbed fast food on the way here.

Nikki stormed off to her room the moment they walked through the front door. He didn't know what Sydney had said to her sister at the crime scene, but anger radiated off the teenager all the way to the duplex. It seemed like an odd reaction, since Sydney had her best interest at heart. But then again, Nikki was at an age when anything could set her off without much provocation.

As he waited for Sydney to finish her own cleanup, he looked around the room. Mail, a laptop and a Bible cluttered the far end of the dining table. A napkin holder and salt and pepper also sat on the table, but it was the well-used Bible that held his interest. He'd never have pegged her for a religious girl back in high school. More of a rebellious troublemaker. Shows how much he didn't know about this woman.

Still limping, she entered the room. Though she wore her soiled uniform, she'd washed away the grime from her face, leaving the anguish from the night even more visible. "Hope you weren't waiting too long."

"No problem," he answered.

"I'll get some sodas." She'd taken out her ponytail, brushed her hair until it gleamed and the full curls swung against her shoulders as she walked.

Even now, worn-out and injured, she was a real beauty. He couldn't help but want to tangle his fingers in the locks to see if they were as soft as they appeared.

Don't go there, Russ.

She returned and set cans of soda on the table. "I'm sorry Nikki ran off to her room."

"Believe me, I understand. My son, Zack, is only seven. He can get mad and storm off in a flash."

"Wait until he's a teenager."

He knew she spoke the truth and that a teen could be problematic, but Russ welcomed the challenge of raising his son at any age.

"I'm not in any way trying to minimize how hard it is to raise your sister," he said. "But if I could have even partial custody of my son, I'd gladly put up with the challenges."

"How long has it been since he's lived with you?"

"Three years," Russ quickly answered and tried to think of a way to move the subject away from Zack. Russ had never told anyone in Logan Lake about his battle with alcohol and losing custody of Zack. He wasn't about to start now.

He reached for his soda. "How long has Nikki been living with you?"

"Let's see." She paused. "She was eight when we left Aunt Lana's house. So almost nine years."

Her wistful tone told him not to pry any deeper. He wouldn't want anyone digging into his past, but something inside—maybe the same desire to see Zack succeed, despite how Russ had screwed things up—made him want these two to do well, so he ignored the warning.

"If you don't mind my asking, what happened to your parents?"

"My father took off when I was fifteen. Said he couldn't be tied down anymore. He promised to keep in touch, but we didn't hear anything about him until he died a few years ago."

"And your mother?"

"She took his leaving hard." Sydney went silent, contemplative, then sighed out what seemed like years of pain. "She started drinking to cover up the pain and spent her days too wasted to take care of us. Right before I turned eighteen, she told me she was going to kick me out and put Nikki up for adoption. I split with Nikki that night and came here to live with Aunt Lana."

All the pain he'd seen reflected in his ex-wife's face when he'd hit rock bottom showed on Sydney's face as she stared into the distance. He took a bite of his sandwich and chewed slowly to give her time to compose herself, but it tasted like sawdust and he washed the bite down with his soda.

He could take her silence no longer. "Want to talk about it?"

"Not really."

"It could help," he murmured softly.

"Or it could put undue focus on the problem."

"Is there still a problem? I mean other than the pain from the past."

She raised the eyebrow near her cut and winced. "You don't give up, do you?"

"Not usually." He smiled but she didn't respond. "I'll stop prying if you want me to."

"No…it's fine. Things with Mom are starting to heat up. After no word from her for years, she contacted me recently and wants to see us. I don't think it's a good idea, but Nikki's all for it. I want what's best for her and that isn't our mother."

"You sound certain about that."

"I am, I mean, I—" She bit her lip, looking uncertain. "I know I'm right, but honestly, I don't know how to handle this with Nikki, so I keep putting it off. I'm hoping she'll forget all about meeting Mom once we move into a real home of our own."

He didn't know how to respond to the problem with her mother, so he focused on the town house. "From everything I've heard it's gonna be a sweet complex when it's finished. Nikki should be real happy there."

"I hope so, but maybe not. I know she'd rather live in a single-family home where she could play her music louder."

Memories of Sydney living with his friend Adam brought a smile to his face. He could still picture her lounging on the sofa, flipping through a magazine, while music blared through the house.

Maybe he could lighten this conversation. "I remember when you liked to crank up your tunes in the summer, and Adam's mom got on your case."

She sighed, a faraway look filling her eyes. "What I wouldn't give for those carefree summers at Aunt Lana's place, when all I thought about were music and boys."

She'd said *boys,* but he knew there had been one boy in particular she'd thought about back then. Him. Now he wondered what would've happened had he pursued those feelings. Would his life have taken a much different road? Maybe he'd never have left Logan Lake to go to Portland. Willie would be alive. Russ wouldn't have hurt the people he loved.

"Don't worry," she said as she peered into his eyes, which he knew exposed his inner turmoil. "I might've had a crush on you, but that was a long time ago. If you can believe it, I'm over you." She offered a smart-aleck grin, washing away his angst.

"Tell me it isn't so." He faked pulling a knife from his chest.

She laughed along with him, lifting his spirits. With their history, he'd thought he'd feel awkward around her. Instead, everything he'd seen so far intrigued him. He wanted to get to know her better. To find out the kind of person she'd become. Especially after the sad story of her parents. She really was fragile and vulnerable, despite the tough exterior she'd tried to portray all night.

Fragile and vulnerable.

Two things that didn't jibe well with being targeted by a murderer. And two things he shouldn't even be thinking about when he felt responsible for keeping this beautiful woman alive.

Sydney peered at Russ's shuttered expression. She'd said something wrong but what, she didn't know. Something special had flashed between them during the light, flirtatious banter. The exact situation she'd hoped for back in high school. Now it felt as if all the light had gone out of him, and he'd put up an invisible barrier.

Just as well. They were law-enforcement officers now, not a couple of teenagers. She wasn't interested in a relationship with another man who'd lead her on, then balk at the responsibility of helping her raise a teen. Relationships were off-limits until Nikki was on her own.

As they finished eating, their conversation drifted back to the case. They rehashed the arrest and murder. Talked about how Garber thought the pictures of the motorcycle would lead somewhere. At

Russ's office tomorrow, they'd transfer them from her phone and enlarge them.

As if on cue, her phone chimed a text.

"Excuse me a minute." She called up the message screen.

You seem to be avoiding my request, Deputy. Maybe I should have a conversation with that cute little sister of yours instead.

"Nikki." Sydney dropped the phone and bolted from the table. "He's after Nikki."

"What?" Russ called after her.

She fled down the hall and shoved open Nikki's door. Hoping to find her sister sitting behind the computer, Sydney stopped short. The room was empty, the window cracked open.

He had her. The killer had her.

Oh, God, no. Please, anything but this. Don't let my baby sister be harmed. Help me find her, please, Lord. Please…

She charged back to the breakfast area and gazed desperately at Russ, who still sat at the table holding her phone. "Nikki's not in her room. The window's open. He must have her."

"You're jumping to conclusions, Syd. Why don't you try calling her?" he said calmly, holding out her phone.

She snatched it and punched in Nikki's speed-dial

number. "Straight to voice mail. What're we gonna do?" Panic seared along her nerve endings.

Russ crossed over to her and placed his hands on her arms. She felt the warmth of his fingers through her sleeves and wished the heat would still the alarm threatening to overwhelm her.

"Take a deep breath and calm down," he said. "It's not likely this creep has Nikki. She's a tough kid. She wouldn't let him take her without making so much noise we would've heard them. Maybe she snuck out."

"She wouldn't do that. Not after I warned her about the killer."

"She's a teenager, Syd. They think they're invincible and do dumb things all the time. We should go to her room and see if we can find a lead."

Sydney jerked away from Russ and raced back down the hall. She heard him follow. In the room, her eyes lit on the computer.

"Her life revolves around her computer. Maybe I can find something there." She dropped into the chair and lifted the lid. After it woke up, Facebook filled the screen, followed by the little chat window with a transcript of a conversation with Emily.

Russ came up behind her and leaned over her shoulder.

Nikki had typed, *Things changed. I can go.*

Emily responded, *Seriously? Thought the warden said you had to stay with her tonight.*

Sydney cringed at the "warden" comment. So

what? She wasn't Nikki's friend or just her sister. She was her legal guardian. For all practical purposes her mother. And mothers had to be wardens at times.

Don't care what she says. I'm going, Nikki added. *It'll be crazy fun. Nick scored two kegs.*

K. Pick me up at the corner so S doesn't see me leave.

Be there in 5, Emily had typed before signing off.

"See," Russ said, his tone meant to soothe but doing nothing to still her anxiety. "She went to a party. Now all we have to do is figure out where they are and bring her home."

It was good to know the killer hadn't abducted Nikki, but his message said he knew she wasn't home. Her life could still be in danger.

A wave of nausea rolled through Sydney's stomach. "The killer's watching us. That's how he knew she snuck out. What if he followed her?"

Russ didn't say anything, but the concern in his eyes said he agreed. "Any idea where the party might be?"

"I'm guessing the pit." She referred to a gravel pit just out of town. "At least that's where most of the parties around here are held."

"Then let's go. We'll issue a BOLO for her friend's car on the way." A Be On the Look Out would alert all officers in the area to watch for Nikki.

"You can call it in while I get my gun. I'll meet you at the car." She didn't wait for agreement but ran to her bedroom, where Nikki had dropped Sydney's backpack after bringing it in from the car.

Sydney jerked out her duty belt and reached for the gun to load it. It wasn't there. She clawed through the pack, came up empty-handed. Her backup gun was here, but her service weapon was missing.

What had happened to it?

It couldn't have fallen out of the bag. Someone had to have taken it. The only person with unrestricted access since Sydney dropped the gun into the backpack was Nikki. She was mad enough about not being able to go to Emily's party to take the gun, just to rile Sydney. Yeah, her sister knew the right buttons to push to make Sydney freak out. This was the exact thing that would do it.

Sydney grabbed her backup gun from the pack. She slipped out of her shirt and removed her bulletproof vest. When she found Nikki alive, and she *would* find her, Nikki would need the vest more than Sydney would.

If the text was true, the killer wanted something from Sydney and he wouldn't kill her until she provided it. Not so with Nikki. He seemed very willing to put a bullet in Nikki to get Sydney to produce this mysterious item.

She slipped the vest on over her shirt then ran for the car. By the time she arrived, Russ had it turned around and the light bar turning.

She jumped in. Before she closed the door, Russ took off. He flipped on the siren and she sat back, finally feeling the strain running had placed on her injured knee. She'd been so consumed with fear for Nikki she hadn't even noticed the pain. Now it throbbed in time with the wails of the siren.

But a little pain didn't matter, Nikki did. And what they both needed right now was God's intervention.

Dear Lord, please wrap Your arms around Nikki and keep her safe. Help us to rescue her and let no one be harmed in the process.

She breathed out her distress and let God's peace take over before opening her eyes.

Russ glanced at her, his eyebrow raised.

"What?" she asked.

"What's with the vest over your shirt?"

She hadn't expected him to question her, but he had to know from when he held her at the murder scene that she'd had the vest on under her shirt, so she explained her reason for the change. "When we get there, you can wait in the car. I'll go in after her."

Russ cocked an eyebrow. "Your logic is full of holes, Syd. Did you take something from Dixon's house?"

"No."

"Then this could just be a ploy to get you out in the open to take you out."

She exhaled sharply. "I'm willing to take that risk to save my sister."

"This's exactly what I was warning you about earlier when you followed Dixon. You have an emotional investment in this. You can't simply bypass everything you've learned about safety and act irrationally."

"Do you have a better idea?"

"We follow protocol and stay together. The area outside the pit is so wide-open we'll be sitting ducks if this guy has a rifle. Our only chance is going in there together and working as a team."

She peered out the window. "It's overcast so that'll help."

"But we're too far from the lake to count on fog hiding us."

"I still think you should stay in the car."

He snorted. "Not a chance."

"I told you—he's not gonna shoot me. He might try to take you out or even Nikki, but not me."

"I'll risk it. I'm not letting you go alone."

She knew by his tight expression that this wasn't negotiable, so she stopped arguing.

"I'll need the phone number from that text so I can have Baker run it down," he said.

She picked up her notebook from the console and jotted it down. She ripped off the paper and gave it to Russ. "We should also check to see if it came from the same phone as the text we received on Dixon's cell."

"I'll have Baker cross-reference it," he answered then fell silent.

She figured he was thinking about how crafty their killer was. Using Dixon's cell when he must have had her phone number, just to add a little more emphasis to the message.

Or maybe the killer used Dixon's cell for another reason?

"You think he sent the message on Dixon's cell to make sure we found the phone?"

"Maybe. Though I don't know why the killer would want us to find Dixon's phone. He might've used it to show us how creative he is. Or maybe he didn't have your cell number yet."

"We may never know." She focused on the road as they neared the pit. She took out her gun. "We should go in silent so we don't scare a bunch of inebriated teens into cars and onto the road."

He flipped off the lights and siren. As they turned onto the driveway, he killed the headlights and slowly drove them to the far end of the lot. He shifted into Park and faced her, uncertainly filling his eyes. "No cars. You think we were wrong?"

"I hope not." She tried to sound confident, but her stomach clenched into a tight ball. Because with no cars in sight, it was unlikely that a party was going on.

Concern for Nikki gnawed at her. She looked away from Russ and sent up a prayer.

If they were wrong, Nikki might have set out for a party somewhere else. Or the killer could already have her and she was at his mercy as he tried to recover something from Sydney that she couldn't possibly produce.

FIVE

Sydney and Russ crept toward the mounds of gravel. As they'd suspected, fog wasn't a factor and the moon had emerged from heavy cloud cover. If the teens were here, they would congregate in the back area of the pit, ringed on three sides by mounds of soil with only one way out.

Worry for Nikki forced Sydney to up her speed, but her feet faltered in deep ruts, slowing her down. She wished a whole cavalry of officers were advancing with them, but they'd agreed not to call in backup, putting other officers in a potential sniper situation. Once they got Nikki out safely, they'd request other units to break up the party.

Finally at the opening, she heard voices and music drifting into the night.

"They *are* here," she whispered to Russ, who stopped next to her.

She peered at a small bonfire casting a flickering light on the group. Approximately twenty-five teens hung in small clusters.

"There's Nikki." She pointed to where her sister, cup in hand, stood talking to Emily.

Russ knelt beside her, and she saw him search the landscape. "Looks like we're alone, but I don't think we should take any chances."

Sydney had almost forgotten about the killer. Seeing Nikki alive and laughing had consumed her thoughts. But Russ was right. They weren't out of the woods yet. Still, she took the time to breathe, slowing her racing pulse. To think this through when all she wanted to do was rush over and throw her arms around her sister. To hold her and plant kisses all over her sweet face.

But that wouldn't teach her what she'd done was wrong. Besides, there was still the issue of the missing gun. And another episode of drinking. Nikki had to learn her actions had consequences. Plus the killer could still end her life if he lurked in the woods.

"I'm going in after her," Sydney said, hating the way her voice wobbled from stress. "Watch our backs. I'll bring her out."

Russ clamped a hand on her arm. "We never agreed to that. I have more experience. I'll go."

Sydney shook off his hand. "We've been through this. You have experience, but the killer would be more than happy to plug you. He wants me alive so I have less to lose."

"I'll cover you." His words came out in a grudging tone, but Sydney had no doubt that he'd do his best to keep her safe.

She gave him a smile, got a flat-lipped one from him. She pushed off and crept to the opening. Once inside the area where walls of gravel kept them out of a shooter's range, she marched into the group.

Nikki's friends looked up. Anxiety spread across their faces.

Good. They *should* be apprehensive.

Sydney was so thankful her sister was alive, but a sudden wave of anger over her taking this chance with her life just to grab a beer made Sydney knock the cup out of Nikki's hand. "You're coming with me."

"Seriously, you didn't come here."

"Seriously, I did." She clamped her hand on Nikki's elbow. "Now come on."

"Later," Nikki said to her friends.

Her friends responded with disappointed goodbyes, but also seemed relieved that Sydney had only come for her little sister and not to break up the party. They'd be sorely disappointed when other officers arrived on the scene to arrest them.

Once outside the group's hearing range, but still in the protective ring of gravel, Sydney took a few deep breaths.

"Where is it?" she demanded.

"Where's what?"

"I know you took my gun."

"What?" Nikki screeched. "I don't have your gun."

"Are you telling me the truth? You didn't take

it from my backpack when I was having dinner with Russ?"

"Why would I want your stupid old gun?" Nikki rolled her eyes.

She wanted to believe Nikki, but she'd lied too often lately. "I hate to do this, but I have to search you."

Nikki glared at her. "Why am I not surprised you don't believe me? You never believe me."

The hurt in Nikki's voice cut to Sydney's core, but she ignored it.

"Lift your arms." She gritted her teeth as she searched.

Nothing in life had prepared her for this. Sure, the academy had taught her how to properly search a suspect, but her sister? How could she pat down her sister without ruining an already deteriorating relationship?

Russ couldn't believe his eyes. Sydney was searching her sister like a common criminal before dressing her in the vest and leading her toward him. He could never imagine treating his son like that. No matter what Zack had done. But then, he couldn't have imagined letting alcohol control his life so he'd lose custody of a child who meant the world to him. So he was in no position to judge Sydney for her actions.

When they reached him, Sydney jerked her head at the car. "I'll take the lead."

She didn't wait for his agreement. He urged Nikki forward with a light hand on her shoulder. She shot him a harsh look but started walking. He saw Sydney check her surroundings. He did the same until they safely reached the car. Sydney grabbed Nikki by the arm and put her into the backseat of the car. She slid into the front and requested units to break up the party.

Russ stood openmouthed and watched.

Was she planning to turn Nikki over to the officers when they arrived? If she wanted Nikki to hate her for life, Sydney was doing the right thing. If not, she was making a colossal mistake. He should know. He was the king of relationship blunders.

But what difference did it make to him? This was her life. Her sister. He was just a fellow officer.

She climbed out of the car and his mind waffled over how he should handle this. Should he tell her what he thought or walk away? Crossing over that professional boundary with Sydney wasn't a good idea. But could he stand by and watch her ruin her relationship with Nikki if he could help?

He groaned and went to her. He'd probably be sorry for trying to butt in, but he had to step in like he'd want someone to do if he were about to make a huge mistake and arrest his son.

"You're not arresting Nikki, are you?" he asked.

"She's lied to me one too many times. Maybe hauling her in for drinking will scare some sense into her."

"Or not."

Her eyes zeroed in on him. "Are trying to tell me how to raise my sister?"

"Wouldn't think of it. Just trying to help you think this through before doing something you might regret later."

She searched his face before she sighed out a long breath. "So what do I do with her? This's the second time I caught her partying. It's got to stop."

"You're certain she was drinking tonight?"

Sydney seemed to think about his question. "I don't know. She had a cup in her hand. We both know she wasn't here long enough to get drunk and she didn't act like it, but why else would she be here?"

Sydney had a point, but it also seemed as if she'd let emotions take over and reacted in haste. "Tell you what…why don't we take her home? I'll administer a breathalyzer. If she's been drinking, I'll talk to her and put the fear of the law into her."

Sydney's jaw tightened. "Why would you do that?"

Why indeed? Because her wounded eyes had kept him from behaving like himself all night. But he wasn't about to admit that. "I've experienced what you're going through and would like to help."

He didn't add that his experience was from the other side of the fence. That he'd lived in the black hole of alcohol dependence for two years and barely escaped alive. That he'd fought hard to reclaim his life and relationship with his son, put his mistakes behind him and come out with regrets he didn't wish on anyone else.

No need to reveal his ugly history. To risk it getting around town and cause the people of Logan Lake to start doubting their police chief. No…not a good idea at all. Especially with a murderer on the loose.

Russ sat back on the sofa in Sydney's family room and let a smile cross his face. He'd spent the past thirty minutes administering the breathalyzer and talking with Nikki. They'd really connected, which totally surprised him. She'd started out belligerent but when he listened to her, she opened up and expressed her frustrations over Sydney not taking the same time to listen.

Now all he needed to do was go out to the garage, tell Sydney that the breathalyzer had come back with a zero reading and discuss Nikki's complaint. Hopefully the two of them would be on the road to better communication by the time this night ended.

He headed for the garage, his steps lighter than they'd been in years with hope trying to ease its way into his heart. Been a long time since he'd hoped for anything. Felt kinda good.

If this was what happened when he opened himself up to others, maybe he should believe what they said at AA about deserving a second chance at life and really start living again.

He passed Nikki coming out of the kitchen with a soda.

"You still here?" she asked, but he heard the humor in her tone. "Thought you'd be out in the garage telling Sydney how great I am and to lighten up."

He laughed. "I'll do that if you remember your promise to talk to her about this."

"I said I would, didn't I?" The good humor disappeared with a shake of her head.

"And if she doesn't hear you right away, don't clam up and take off."

She stalked across the room. "*Or* if she does something so lame again, like accusing me of taking her stupid old service weapon."

Hold up. Was Sydney's gun missing? If so, it explained why Sydney had patted Nikki down. He wondered if that was the real reason she hadn't been carrying at the town house. Then again...she'd had a gun at the gravel pit. But it could be her backup.

He hated to think she might have lied to him at the town houses when she told him she'd left her service weapon in the car. He was a good judge of character. Lying didn't fit what he knew of Sydney. But it did fit a teenager.

"Did you take her gun?" he called after Nikki.

She stopped and looked back at him. "If you have to ask, you're as lame as she is." Shaking her head, she went down the hallway.

Despite the return of her attitude, he had to say

he believed her. She sounded convincing. Plus he hadn't seen Sydney pull a gun from Nikki during her search. After he told Sydney about the breathalyzer, he would ask about the gun.

He went to the garage and found her lying on her stomach in the front seat of her cruiser, digging under the passenger's seat.

"Syd," he called out.

She snapped up, banging her head on the steering wheel and groaning.

"Sorry," he said. "I didn't mean to startle you like that." He handed her the breathalyzer case. "The test read zero."

"She wasn't drinking."

"Not a drop."

"Then why was she at the party?" She set the breathalyzer kit on the seat.

"She wants to tell you about it. If you'll listen."

When Sydney's eyes narrowed, Russ took a step back. This was probably the same look she used on traffic stops. Very effective.

"Did Nikki tell you I don't listen?" she asked, her tone testy. "I listen all the time."

"Like tonight? When you patted her down and threw her in the back of your car without letting her explain?"

Pain swept over Sydney's face. He shouldn't have been so direct. He knew how hard it was to be a parent. His wife had left him and taken Zack when he was too deep in the bottle to be a good father, so who was he to accuse Sydney of anything?

He gazed into her eyes. Eyes that were older than her years, as if they'd seen far too much trouble in her young life. But they were also compelling and deep enough to drown in, if he ever let himself take a plunge.

"I'm sorry, Syd. I should never have said that. I know how hard it is to raise a seven-year-old boy. It's gotta be even harder to parent a teenager... I could never do what you're doing."

"I appreciate your apology." Her voice thick with emotion, she looked off into the distance.

He caught a glimpse of disappointment before she turned away.

Was she disappointed in herself or in him for questioning her? If he told her about his failure with Zack maybe that would help. Or would it just blur the lines of professionalism between them that he couldn't seem to stay behind? It was better to leave before he confided his problems and involved her in his personal mess.

"I'll get someone to drop off my car so you can have that talk with Nikki." He dug out his phone and pressed Garber's speed-dial number.

"It'll take a few minutes for someone to get here, so why don't we wait inside?" Her lips turned up in an endearing smile, making him want to be on the receiving end of smiles like this more often.

He stood there basking in the warmth. Letting the

strong connection settle over him and watching her eyes transmit a flash of interest.

"You there, Chief?" Garber's voice coming over the phone turned her eyes shy. She spun and went to the door.

He eased out a breath and put the phone to his ear. "Any word on the lights?"

"Not yet."

"I need someone to drop off my cruiser at Deputy Tucker's house." He shook his head and watched Sydney enter the house.

He'd told himself to treat her just like one of his men and not to let his awareness of her as a woman muddy the waters. This shouldn't be such a complicated thing. Especially when he knew better than to lead her on. No woman deserved to get involved with him after the way he'd failed his ex.

"It might take a while," Garber said. "Most of the guys are processing the kids from the party."

"Just get it here as soon as you can." Russ disconnected and contemplated staying in the garage. Not a good idea, because Sydney would come looking for him.

He went inside and found her sitting in the family room, sipping a glass of water.

She held it up. "You want anything?"

He shook his head and took a seat as far away from her as possible.

"I've been thinking about what you said." She shifted on the sofa. "You were right. I *have* been jumping down Nikki's throat lately and not listening to her. I'll have to work on how I react from now on."

"Good." He let that warm feeling from helping slide over him like a soft blanket.

She set her glass on the table. "Not that there's any excuse for how I've been treating her, but when I caught her drinking I lost it. Our mother was a mean drunk—" she shuddered "—and I don't want Nikki to follow in her footsteps, so I overreacted."

All hope that had raised his spirits earlier flooded out. She'd said *drunk* with more disgust than he'd ever heard in the word. It felt like a slap in the face.

Sure, his ex had called him a drunk many times, with great passion, but not like this. So much for thinking he deserved a second chance at a normal life. He'd wrecked his life, and second chances didn't come easy.

Had she said something wrong, or did Russ go hot and cold like this all the time? If so, life around him would never be dull. Not that she was planning life around him. Especially after his comment in the garage about never being able to raise a teenager like she was doing. He was just like all the other guys her age—didn't want a teen to tie them down.

She wanted to be disappointed in him, but honestly, she could understand why a guy wouldn't want the extra responsibility. She loved her sister, but there were days when she'd be happy to live like other women her age.

Still, she could imagine one day staring across the table at his compelling eyes. Eyes that had locked on hers in the garage, kicking up her pulse. Blue eyes that narrowed as they roamed the room, as if searching for a way out.

"You okay?" she asked.

"Tired."

"I hear you." She regretted that after all they'd shared tonight they were heading toward inconsequential small talk.

He stood. "I can wait for my ride on the porch."

"That's not necessary."

"Nikki wants to talk to you," he said.

"She won't be going to bed anytime soon."

"Still, I should go." He headed to the door.

"Well, then, thanks again for talking to Nikki. I hope she didn't tell you any deep, dark family secrets." She grinned to lighten the mood but when he didn't return it, she took a sip of water.

His face turned even more serious. "It's really none of my business, but did you lose your service weapon?"

She choked on her water and coughed until her throat cleared.

"I'll take that to mean you did."

She guzzled more water and fought for calm. She wanted to trust the caring expression he'd trained on her earlier, to confide in him about her missing gun, but she couldn't tell him before her sergeant. As her boss, he deserved a heads-up before her carelessness made it onto the town's gossip chain.

Anyway, she still hoped a more thorough search than the quick one she'd just done in her car would produce the weapon.

"Sydney?" Russ's tone grew more insistent.

When her phone chimed a text, she nearly praised God aloud for the timely interruption. "Excuse me a minute." She called up the message.

Your sister may have gotten home safe tonight, Deputy, but tomorrow's another day. Give back what you took or both of you will pay.

"What is it?" Russ asked. "What's wrong?"

"It's from him again." She handed the phone to Russ and fought for control over the fear spearing her stomach. "Why is he doing this? I didn't take anything."

Russ's expression darkened. "More pressing for me at the moment is the fact that he knows Nikki's home."

Sydney had been so busy thinking about the item she'd supposedly taken from Dixon's house and what the man who wanted it could do to her sister that she hadn't questioned how he knew Nikki's whereabouts.

Her heart sank. "He's still watching us."

"It's very likely. You need to show these messages to Nikki so she sees the full magnitude of the situation."

"I can't… I've already scared her. This'll terrify her even more."

"She needs to know this guy means business." He clenched his jaw. "We can't have her taking off again."

"I need some time to think about the best way to handle this, Russ. I can't decide just like that." She snapped her fingers.

"Fine. You think on it, but while you're doing that, I'm arranging for a protection detail for tonight. And think about moving to a safe house tomorrow."

"I don't think that's necessary," she protested.

"The killer's messages are clear, Syd. He's not about to stop until he gets what he wants." He planted his feet and trained a steely gaze on her.

She didn't know what to do. She couldn't think with his eyes drilling into her like this. "Make the arrangements—for an outside detail only. I don't want anyone in the house until I decide what to tell Nikki."

He headed for the door then spun, facing her with a grave expression. "I get that you're trying not to scare Nikki, but you need to prepare her for what could happen if this escalates."

Numb, Sydney watched him leave. What would she say to Nikki? How did she tell her kid sister that she might have to go into hiding because a killer had threatened her life?

SIX

The next morning, Sydney laid her Bible on the table and stretched. After a restless night, her morning devotion had given her hope and reminded her that God was in control of their lives.

"Just remember that, Sydney," she said as she crossed the room. "Even if this day doesn't go according to plan."

She peeked through the blinds as she'd periodically done throughout the night when she couldn't sleep from worrying about the killer and over losing her gun. A few times, she'd actually been thankful to have the distraction of the missing gun to keep her mind off the killer.

After Russ left last night, she'd thoroughly searched the interior of her car and confirmed there'd been no forced entry of the vehicle. So if someone stole the gun while she was on the hill, then the thief had used a slim jim, leaving no evidence behind. But if they were after weapons, why hadn't they taken her shotgun and her backup gun, too? It was almost as if whoever took it knew she'd get in trouble for losing her service weapon and had done it more for that reason than to possess a gun.

So who could that be? Was there someone in her department who wanted her gone because she was a woman? She'd had her share of issues over being female, but she didn't think things had reached that level. However, she couldn't dismiss the possibility that maybe she'd overlooked something. She'd have to be on alert for another deputy who seemed bitter toward her. Maybe once she told Krueger about the missing gun, he'd shed some light on the problem.

She sighed and peered at Russ's cruiser. At least she had a bed to toss and turn in. He only had a car. He'd arrived sometime between two and three in the morning, parked in the driveway and spelled his other officer. She'd thought about telling him he could come in and bunk on the sofa, but after the way she'd responded to him last night, she didn't think that was such a good idea.

Now guilt from making him stay out in the cold had her marching out the door to invite him to breakfast.

The gray clouds had split wide this morning, letting the sun's warm rays bring relief from the drizzly rain. Still the grass and driveway glistened with moisture. She was careful not to slip on mossy patches courtesy of a few months of steady rain.

She glanced up to find Russ had climbed from his car and leaned on the open door in a relaxed stance. When their eyes met, a fluttery sensation in her stomach brought all the feelings she had had for him as a teen flooding back. And yet they weren't the same. More intense, actually.

"Everything okay?" His voice was warm and sleepy as his gaze drifted lazily over her.

She forced her mind off his perusal. "I'm sorry I was so closed-minded last night. Would you like to come in for some breakfast? We can talk about what to do next."

"Sounds good." He closed his car door.

Acutely aware that he was following her, she led the way into her house.

"Coffee?" she asked outside the kitchen.

"That would be great." He took a seat in the same chair as last night and stretched, drawing his uniform shirt tight across his wide chest.

As she went into the kitchen to prepare a tray, she remembered the feeling of security he'd provided last night when he'd held her. The warmth of his body easing out the cold. She'd been alone for so long, carrying the responsibility of raising Nikki, that it would be so great to find a man to share the burden.

"Enough daydreaming, Sydney," she whispered. "No man wants that kind of responsibility."

Finishing the tray, she went back to the dining area and hoped he was in the mood to listen. A night in a cold car wasn't likely in her favor. She found him stretching and bending as if sleeping in the cold had kinked his muscles.

"I'm really sorry you had to spend the night outside." She set a cup of coffee in front of him.

"Not a problem. That's my job." He picked up the mug and took a few careful sips of the steaming liquid. "This will keep me awake until I can grab a quick shower and another gallon of coffee."

He offered a crooked grin, so like that of the boy she'd hoped would smile at her this way. She didn't know how to respond and simply dropped onto the chair while pointing at blueberry bagels.

He split one open.

"Any new developments on the case overnight?" She took a long sip, savoring the nutty flavor of her fresh-ground coffee.

He glanced up. The teenager's grin was long gone. "A few. We confirmed the weapon used was a nine-millimeter. Not that this will help a lot. With so many people owning nines these days, that really doesn't narrow things down." He set the mug down and traced the rim with his forefinger. "Baker confirmed the two texts came from the same phone number. Phone company identified it as a prepaid. We're tracking down registration details, but I'm not holding out hope it'll be legit."

"So what happens next?"

"Garber will look at your pictures. We'll interview Dixon's boss and coworkers."

"I'm looking forward to talking to the foreman,"

she said. "It might just be a coincidence that Dixon worked on the town-house construction site, but I don't think so."

He nodded his agreement and took another sip of coffee.

This seemed like a perfect time to broach the subject of a protective detail. She set down her cup and took a deep breath. "Before we get going I wanted to talk about plans for our protection."

"I haven't changed my mind about the detail if that's what you're hoping."

"Not exactly. Just thinking we could compromise."

He lifted an eyebrow and sat back. "I'm listening."

"Since I'll be spending the day with you anyway, Nikki is really the only one who needs someone with her. I showed her the text messages and she agreed to let an officer accompany her to school." Sydney smiled. "She said it might even be cool to have her own personal bodyguard."

"That works for me."

"There's one more thing…"

He groaned and leaned forward again. "I knew this was too easy."

"I have to see Krueger before my day starts. I'll be happy to let you follow me to the office if you want, but I don't want you sitting in the parking lot waiting for me."

"You'll have another deputy accompany you on the drive to my office?" he asked.

"If that's the only way you'll agree to this, then, yes."

He met her gaze, his softening. "You may think I'm insensitive, Syd, but I get that you don't want to look weak around your coworkers. I've worked with enough women in this business to know you're held to higher standards." His eyes narrowed. "But first and foremost, I want to make sure you're safe. And this guy has proven that he knows what he's doing."

"I appreciate all you're doing, Russ, really I do." She let her eyes remain glued to his and hoped her sincerity shone through. "I worked so hard to be respected as a fellow officer. Even if I'm a rookie with a lot to learn, I don't want this incident to cause a setback."

"I can understand that." He lifted the cup to his lips.

She didn't see a smirk or any other evidence that he was humoring her, but only time would tell. For now, they'd made an uneasy peace. Hopefully nothing would happen today to take it away.

Sydney stood in front of Krueger in his office. Before the door closed behind her, he'd told her that he didn't like how she'd wormed her way onto the investigative team. She didn't correct him, but did update him on the investigation and listened as he gave her instructions to report in on a regular basis.

And with the sergeant already miffed at her, she then had to tell him about losing the gun. She'd expected him to erupt like a volcano, but he sat behind his pristine desk, long jaw clenched and eyes narrowed in hard little slits.

His intense scrutiny made her squirm but she refused to fall apart. Last night she'd acted like a helpless baby, but she'd reclaimed the strength that had abandoned her at the sight of Carl Dixon's body. Her talk with Russ gave her the confidence to withstand Sarge's glare. She'd wait him out.

Just as she was ready to say something, he shoved his chair back and stood, towering over her. "This why you weren't carrying last night?"

"No!" She paused to let her shrill tone return to normal. "I left the gun in my backpack like I told you."

He trained a glare on her that would make an innocent person admit to a crime. "It's one thing to lose a gun. Another to cover it up."

Her temper spiked at his insinuation. "I'm not covering anything up. The gun was in my backpack."

"Fine, but if I find out you've been playing me, I'll have your job." His glare diminished a bit.

Hoping this was over, she started backing away.

"Hold on. I'm not done with you yet." He tilted his bald head to the side. "You do realize I'll have to write you up for this?"

"No." She clenched her hands. "I mean, no, sir, I

wasn't certain you'd have to do that, but I understand your position."

"See that you do understand how serious this is. Don't let it happen again. And don't go blabbing about this to Chief Morgan." He exhaled. "Maybe we can keep this mark on our department's integrity from spreading through the community."

"Yes, sir," she said as a rush of heat flooded her face. She hated that her actions tarnished the team's solid reputation.

"I'll authorize a new duty weapon for you, but you better search a little harder for the missing one. How you can lose a gun is beyond me." He jerked his head toward the door. "Now get outta here and see that you don't lose this one."

Face still flaming, she bolted for the door. Once out of view, she stopped to gain her composure before picking up her new duty weapon.

She wasn't surprised Sarge wanted to keep this quiet. There was a lot of competition between the sheriff's department and Logan Lake P.D. Letting Russ find out about the missing gun could make Sarge look bad, and if she'd learned anything in her first year on the job, it was not to let the big guy down. Too bad she couldn't seem to accomplish that goal this week.

Russ held open the front door. He'd had enough of City Council Chairman Fred Windsor offering advice on how to handle this case. The man had hired Russ and he, along with the council, served as Russ's supervisor, but Windsor didn't have a clue as to the intricacies of running a murder investigation. Which Russ had told the man for the past thirty minutes.

"See that you keep me informed, Chief," Windsor commanded. "We can't have our citizens afraid to leave their homes."

"Will do." Russ pushed the door open wider to encourage the man to leave.

"You have my cell number," Windsor said. "If you need to consult on the murder, don't be too proud to use it." Windsor slapped his meaty palm into Russ's hand, then exited the building.

The councilman paused and turned, but before he said anything else, Russ walked away. He wound his way through the squad room that was so different from the busy Portland office. Logan Lake employed only a handful of officers, forcing each one to wear many hats. If this investigation didn't end quickly, he'd have to request additional help from county. That idea sat as well with him as the thought of consulting with Windsor.

At Garber's desk, Russ waited while the officer finished his phone call with the president of the local dirt-bike club. After breakfast, Sydney had given him her phone's memory card and he'd printed out photos. The first three digits of the dirt bike's license plate were clear as a bell, confirming this bike as the one their killer rode. But with only three digits, a DMV search would return thousands of vehicles and take forever to run down.

Garber recognized the cycle as a BMW, and since very few people in the area could afford a twenty-thousand-dollar bike, they would focus on the bike itself.

Garber hung up. "I was wrong. There're a few more of these bikes in the county than I thought, but Larry gave me a list of owners so I can follow up."

"Good. That's the first solid lead we have. Anything else happen while I was with Windsor?"

"Baker asked if you'd stop in." He nodded toward the conference room. "He's still talking to the girl."

"Let me know what you turn up on the bikes." Russ clapped Garber on the back before heading down the hallway.

This teenage girl had showed up earlier claiming she'd attended the party where Dixon plied Sydney's sister with alcohol. And the girl claimed she had information to help with this investigation. Russ wanted to talk with her, but then Windsor had shown up and Russ had passed her off to Baker.

The girl slouched so far down in the chair he thought she might slide off. Dressed in a revealing V-neck shirt, skinny jeans and high-top sneakers, she had eyes glazed with drug use.

"Chief," Officer Baker said and nodded at the girl. "Rachelle, go ahead and tell the chief what you told me about Dixon's arrest."

The girl picked at her purple fingernails. "After

Nikki's sister slapped the cuffs on the dude, she went all kamikaze on him. Gettin' in his face and yelling that if he ever came near Nikki again, she'd kill him." She paused as if she'd dropped some big bombshell.

"And then what happened?" Russ asked.

"Well, nothing, but, I mean, she was really mad. I thought she might kill him right there." She sat up a bit. "So when I heard he was dead, I figured she did it."

"That it?" Russ asked Baker.

He nodded and added a knowing look that Russ didn't like.

"Outside," Russ commanded. When they both moved into the hallway, Russ jerked the door closed. "You really think Deputy Tucker offed Dixon?"

Baker shrugged. "Maybe. At least it's possible. I'm not sure what I would've done if Dixon had taken advantage of someone in my family like that."

Russ ran a hand around the back of his neck. Maybe he needed to give the reasoning more thought. If he were in her situation and he'd caught Zack drinking, what would he have done? A boy wasn't as vulnerable to a predator like Dixon, but still, Russ wouldn't want anyone to expose his son to drugs and alcohol, and Russ would make sure the creep who did so paid. But how far would he go?

Actually, the most important question here was how far would—did—Sydney go? Maybe Sydney *was* in on what went down last night. Maybe the killer was planning to take her out not for what she saw, but because she was part of the operation. Maybe…but his gut told him otherwise.

Still, he had a job to do. That included following this investigative avenue. "I'm not liking her for this, but follow it up. Keep it between you and me for now."

"You got it," Baker said.

"And follow up on this girl. Let's see if she has any connection with Dixon and if this impromptu interview is her way of trying to cover it up."

"Right." Baker spun and returned to the room.

His mood somber, Russ headed back toward his office. At the end of the hallway, he spotted Sydney coming through the door, dressed in a clean, well-fitting uniform that emphasized the length of her fantastic legs. A few long strides took her into the bull-pen area.

Garber and Officer Plank stood near their cubicles. As they followed her progress, their gazes filled with appreciation. She offered them a passing smile as if she didn't see the fuss she was creating.

Russ wanted to yell at his men for acting like teenage boys, but what good would that do? Even with the strain of the night lingering on her face, she was a gorgeous woman. Tan, smooth skin. Eyes wide with long lashes. He couldn't make his men not look at her. But he wanted to. More than he cared to admit.

Garber tossed out a lame pickup line. Russ chewed

on the inside of his mouth to keep from saying something. Sydney laughed and fired back a comment that confirmed she was used to this kind of situation. A rookie in law enforcement, she wasn't a rookie in dealing with unwanted male attention.

In the hours he'd sat outside her house last night, he'd cemented in his mind his decision to keep their interaction professional. He couldn't let the mere sight of her derail his plan. He certainly didn't want to end up sporting the same goofy look that was plastered on Garber's face. He'd start by asking about her threat to Dixon.

He took a defensive stance and steeled his mind for her arrival.

"Something wrong?" she asked when she came closer than he'd have liked.

"Tell me about threatening Dixon the night you arrested him."

"Can we do this somewhere more private?" She tipped her head to the side.

He followed her gaze and found his men still gawking at her. He tossed a glare their way and they scattered.

"Let's go to my office."

When she sat and crossed those legs that went on for miles, he perched on the side of his desk and waited to hear her explanation.

"You don't really think I killed Dixon, do you?"

This wasn't how he'd expected her to start. "You

didn't tell me last night that you threatened the guy, so what am I supposed to think?"

"I just needed to blow off some steam. After I yelled at him, I forgot all about it." She sighed. "I shouldn't have lost my cool on the job, but I didn't kill him."

"What about that unresolved issue from last night? You ready to tell me about your service weapon?"

A brief flash of unease crossed her face before she controlled it. "My gun's right here." She clapped a hand on her holster. "Would you like to see it?"

He should trust her, but her expression said she was keeping something from him. It might not have anything to do with this case or it might have everything to do with it, but he knew actually asking to see the weapon would do more harm than good in their working relationship.

If she was going to confide in him, she needed to trust him, so he'd drop the subject for now. "I'll take your word for it."

She seemed to sag in relief.

Yeah, he was on-target here. She might not have killed Dixon, but something was going on with her that she didn't want him to know about. He was more determined than ever to ferret out the truth. No matter how long it took.

SEVEN

Facing Russ across his desk, Sydney rested her hands on the desktop as he clicked on his computer keyboard, opening the other pictures from her phone. He'd accepted her answer about her gun, but his eyes said he wasn't letting the issue go.

She hated not telling him the truth. She hadn't technically lied to him, as the gun in her holster was a service weapon, but it was a lie of omission, nonetheless. She only hoped that news of her missing gun didn't get out, as she'd hate to have to tell him why she hadn't been forthcoming.

"Here we go." Russ pointed at his monitor.

She leaned closer to look at the first picture of Dixon's street.

"See anything?" Russ asked.

"Nothing worth killing me for," she answered.

He clicked to the next picture. They studied the version nearly identical to the first. He clicked again. Same scenario.

He tilted his head sideways. She spotted a small

scar on his chin that she'd not noticed before. He didn't have this scar back in high school. She'd spent four summers studying everything about him. She would've seen it.

Odd that she hadn't noticed it last night. Or this morning at breakfast.

Maybe it was visible now because he'd shaved since she'd last seen him or because she was so close to him. Close enough to catch the lingering fragrance from his minty soap. So masculine and appealing, her attraction to him magnified tenfold.

"Is something wrong?" she heard Russ ask, but she didn't want to break the moment just yet.

"Syd?"

"What? Oh, no. Just thinking." She stabbed a finger at the photo on the screen. "That's the girl who took off when I arrived. Might help to ID her."

"I'll print this out so we can follow up." As he turned back to the monitor, his gaze slid over her, telling her he'd noticed her discomfort. His lips curved in that cocky smile she found irresistible.

Well, she'd resist it. At least she'd do her best. The last thing she needed right now was to fall for another guy who'd bail on her. She needed to keep her focus on the work.

"I got your fax." Russ lifted copies of the arrest reports she'd sent to him when she'd stopped to talk with Sarge. "Nothing glaringly obvious in here, but I already have one of my men following up with the people you arrested. Maybe one of the teens' parents had the same reaction as you did to the judge's sentence and decided to take things into their own hands."

"I'm not really sure how that would explain the texts asking for the item from Dixon's house. Still, it's a lead we can't ignore."

He went to retrieve pictures of the girl from his printer and stood looking down on Sydney. "I've scheduled a meeting so we can bring everyone on the team up to speed and reassign as necessary. I'm assuming you'll want to join us."

She nodded.

"Then follow me." He spun on his heels.

She didn't know what was up with the formal tone he'd adopted since she'd arrived today, but it was good that he didn't seem to be aware of her as a woman. This would only help them focus.

He took long strides down the hall. He was nearly six feet tall and she had a hard time keeping up. It was almost as if he was trying to run away. Maybe he'd detected her interest in him and he was trying to run from her, as he had in high school.

He abruptly peeled off left and into a room where three officers were seated at a long table. They didn't seem surprised to see her, so he must have informed them she'd be representing the county on this case. No one looked particularly angry to see her here, but the room was thick with tension.

"Everyone, this is Deputy Tucker." Russ motioned for her to sit.

She nodded her greeting, then chose a spot at the end of the table where she could clearly see everyone without having to swivel her chair.

"Okay," Russ said. "Let's go down the line. Give updates on your assignments. Be sure to start with your name for Sy—Deputy Tucker."

Sydney saw a few eyes widen at Russ's near slip of her name, but no one commented.

"I'm Bill Garber," the officer to Russ's right said. "We met in the bull pen." He stood and winked at her.

She felt her face flush over the reference to the way he'd tried to pick her up out there. She willed it to stop, but the heat flooded all the way to the top of her head.

He tacked up photos of Dixon on the board. "We've run the vic's background. He's from Portland. Haven't located any family yet, but he was on the P.D.'s narcotics radar." He glanced back at the other officers. "He's never been arrested by them, but Portland P.D. agreed to follow up with his known associates. Anything worthy of our attention and they'll contact me."

"What about his rental house?" Russ asked.

"The state crime-lab investigators will arrive in a few hours. After they finish the murder scene, they'll move on to his house. I'm still following up on the dirt-bike lead. You all have the photos of the bike.

We've issued a BOLO." He scrubbed a hand across his face. "I haven't had as much luck with the cell phone the texts originated from. It's a prepaid registered to a Portland address, so I have Portland P.D. working on it and hope to know more later today."

"Keep up the good work, Garber." Russ's honest praise was refreshing to see. Sarge never told the deputies they were doing a good job, just found ways they could do better. "Okay, next."

"Officer Baker," the man next to Garber said. "I'm making progress on Dixon's phone log. Dixon received numerous calls from the same number as the texts. Should finish running down the rest of the calls by afternoon." He paused to take a deep breath. "I'm also working through the list of students present at Dixon's first arrest. I'll be interviewing the parents this afternoon to see if any of them decided to take action for Dixon supplying their kid with alcohol." He let a knowing look settle on Sydney.

So this was where Russ got the info that she'd threatened Dixon. She wouldn't justify this allegation with a response.

"Good." Russ clapped his hands together. "So it looks like we're moving along. Deputy Tucker and I'll head out to the town houses to talk with the construction foreman and Dixon's coworkers." He handed the photos he'd printed to Garber. "These are shots outside Dixon's house from the night of his drug bust. Anyone recognize the girl?"

Garber studied the photos and passed them down

the line. Each officer looked at them then gave negative responses.

He held up his hand when the third officer tried to give back the photos. "See if the principal at the school can ID this girl." He clapped his hands. "I don't have to tell you this's a priority, but we still need to keep up with the regular workload. So make sure you balance the two without breaking my overtime budget."

As the meeting broke up, Sydney watched Russ interact with his men. Though they'd just discussed murder, once the official meeting ended they'd taken on a familial kind of easiness, with Russ assuming the role of the father figure. It was easy to see the respect they held for him—an admiration far different from the deference Sarge demanded from the deputies who served under him.

She loved her job, but hadn't realized until now how much better it would be with a leader devoted to making the men the best they could be. Russ was that kind of leader. She imagined he was probably that kind of father. Maybe that kind of life partner...

She watched him and wondered why his marriage broke up. Had he been the cause of the breakup? If so, what had he done?

Seriously, what difference did it make?

As she came to know the upstanding man he'd become, her attraction went beyond his good looks. But that wouldn't change the fact that Nikki still needed her, and Russ had been clear last night when he said he couldn't handle raising a teen.

She sighed. Russ met her gaze with a questioning one of his own. She shrugged to tell him not to worry about her. But his knowing look told her he wouldn't give up that easily on finding out what was bothering her.

Yes, he was a man who cared. A man who right now seemed as if he cared too much for his own good. Maybe hers, too.

Russ didn't know what had happened at the meeting to make Sydney clam up, but she'd been too quiet for his liking on the drive to the town houses. She seemed to be brooding about something ever since he caught her sighing at the end of the meeting. He'd opted to respect her privacy so far, but this might have to do with the case. He had so little to go on that he had to ask what was troubling her.

"It's not like you to be so quiet." He gave her an encouraging smile and returned his focus to the road. "What's going on?"

From the corner of his eye, he saw her shrug.

"Same shrug as in the conference room," he said. "If you're holding something back about this investigation, I hope you'll change your mind and tell me about it."

She looked away. "There's nothing you need to know."

"So have you gone back to feeling guilty about Dixon?"

She groaned. "You don't give up, do you?"

"That's what made me such a good homicide detective," he said with a wink.

She shifted to face him. "If you were so good at it why'd you leave?"

He shook his head. "Oh, no, you don't. We were talking about you, not me."

"Now who doesn't want to talk?"

He slowed at the stop sign and looked at her. "You tell me what's bothering you. I'll tell you why I left Portland."

"You first."

"Uh-uh. You go first or we don't have a deal."

"Fine." She sighed. "It's really no big deal. I was a little jealous over how well your team works together. Sarge doesn't encourage teamwork. He calls all the shots, and we can't question anything."

This wasn't at all what he'd expected her to say. "Are you unhappy in your job?"

"Unhappy? No…I like it. I'm just saying I would work better under your style of management than Sarge's. But I guess that's the only way he can operate."

"Too many years in the military to roll any other way." Nearing the crime scene, Russ turned on his blinker. "I can tell you I've never seen another P.D. where everyone calls the commanding officer Sir. In most places that'd peeve the commander."

"Actually, I don't mind that. Makes me remember I'm a rookie and still have a lot to learn so I can be the best deputy I can be."

"Never imagined you'd end up in law enforcement. At least from the arresting side of the coin."

"Thanks a lot." She shot a playful punch to his arm.

He faked an injured look. "I'm just saying you were a bit rebellious in high school."

"Only in my looks and maybe my smart mouth, but once I found God, I'd never do anything to break the law."

"You and religion. That's another story I need to hear." He swung into the parking lot.

He expected her to clam up or demand his reason for leaving Portland before giving him any other information, but she smiled and took a deep breath. "Coming to faith is a story I'll gladly share. One day my mom was so mad at Nikki for spilling milk that she threatened to give her away." She shuddered. "I thought she'd really do it. I panicked. Called 911."

He shifted into Park and watched her face contort with pain. His heart ached with the desire to remove it, but he knew from dealing with his ex-wife that nothing he could say would ever take away the heartache caused by an alcoholic in a drunken spree.

He also knew from AA that talking about the pain helped. She didn't have to be a recovering alcoholic to benefit from the principle.

He swiveled to face her and gave her an encouraging smile. "How old were you?"

"I was sixteen. Nikki was almost three."

"Must have been hard on both of you."

"It was, but the officer who responded to the call helped us. In fact, she changed our lives." A gentle smile graced her lips. "Vicki—the officer—called social services, but she knew since this was the first report they'd probably give my mom the benefit of the doubt. They did. But Vicki didn't leave it at that. She told me about her church and asked if it would be okay if she arranged for Nikki to go to preschool there for free while I was in school. So I didn't have to worry about her staying with my mom."

"That was a very generous offer."

She gave a vigorous nod. "What I didn't know at the time was that Vicki paid Nikki's tuition, not the school. I'd pick Nikki up after school and started hanging out at the church. Through the generosity of the people there, Nikki and I both came to know God."

"This's why you went into law enforcement."

"I want to give back the same way Vicki gave to us."

Russ let the warmth of her soft smile chase years of darkness from his heart. He'd only spent a short while with her, but could already tell she was a special woman. A woman he was as attracted to now as he had been in college. Maybe more so. But also a woman who deserved someone who wouldn't hurt her any more than she'd been hurt so far.

As their eyes met, the same feeling charged between them as last night. He wished he was the guy for her, but he wasn't. Never would be.

Sydney had done it again, but she didn't know what *it* was. Russ seemed so open for a while, but now he'd closed down tighter than Fort Knox. She hoped he would ease up when they talked with the foreman and Dixon's coworkers.

As they climbed the hill toward the area not cordoned off by crime-scene tape, the rapid fire of pneumatic nail guns filled the crisp fall air. Their feet crunched over colorful fallen leaves. Sydney couldn't help but contrast the fresh feeling of the day with the terror she'd felt in this same location last night. She followed Russ's confident stride up the hill. He gave her hope that he could put an end to this mess.

The crew was confined to one small area in the middle of the site, where they worked on framing garages. Russ and Sydney found the supervisor and pulled him aside. Sydney didn't miss the workers' skeptical gazes fixed on her as she passed. But she could handle it. She'd dealt with men on the street who'd tested her resolve on the job. This wasn't any different.

Russ introduced himself to the supervisor and offered his hand.

"Nate Johnson," the man responded.

"Tell us about your relationship with Dixon," Russ said.

"Not much to tell. He wasn't an ideal employee. Came in late, liked to take long breaks. But when he did work, he framed faster than any of my other men, so he made up for the slacking off."

"We noticed on Dixon's phone logs that he called you quite often."

"Like I said—he was a slacker. Kept trying to make excuses about missing work. I put up with it because of his skills, but once we finished framing, I knew I'd have let him go."

"Dixon know that?"

He shrugged. "Not likely. The guy lived in the moment, ya know?"

"Can you think of anyone who might want to kill him?"

He shook his head. "Nah. He wasn't a real stand-up kinda guy, but he was well liked around here."

Russ nodded. "Anyone in particular he hung around with?"

"Dixon and Eustis were pretty thick."

"Eustis here today?" Russ asked.

Johnson jerked his head toward one of the men. "The one with the red bandana."

Sydney followed his line of sight and found the guy watching them, his gaze uncertain. A quick glance at Russ told her he'd seen the same nervousness on Eustis's face.

Russ pulled out a folded copy of the picture of the motorcycle. "You recognize this bike?"

Johnson took off his gloves, tucked them in the back pocket of his overalls then took the paper. "Yeah. Belongs to Eustis."

She and Russ swung their gazes to Eustis. His eyes flashed open. He searched the area then back-pedaled slowly as his expression turned wary.

"He's gonna run," Sydney said and took off in his direction.

She raced across the hilly terrain, Russ's footfalls pounding down the hill toward the parking lot. If she didn't catch Eustis, Russ would cut him off before he could reach his vehicle.

Pain from her knee shot up her leg, but she ignored it. Eustis was quick, but with heavy boots weighing him down, she gained on him. Just as he would dart into the lot, she launched her body from above and tackled him.

He landed hard, but his body cushioned her fall. Adrenaline giving her strength, she pressed her good knee into his back and dragged his hands behind his back then cuffed them.

"Good work, Syd." Russ came up beside her, breathing hard.

She shrugged it off, even though his praise meant a great deal to her.

"I mean it. Really good work. There are seasoned officers who wouldn't have picked up on the guy's signals." Russ grabbed Eustis's arms, and together they hefted him to his feet.

The other workers came down the hill and stood watching the two cops haul off their coworker. Their faces held a measure of respect instead of the patronizing stares she'd gotten earlier. She'd redeemed herself a bit, but the guilt over failing last night when a life hung in the balance managed to overshadow it.

Russ put Eustis in the backseat. "We might as well head straight to county."

Everyone arrested in the city was processed through county, but Russ could've taken Eustis back to his office to question him first. She didn't know why he was passing up that opportunity, but she wouldn't question him in front of Eustis. So she settled back and rode in silence.

When they arrived at her office, Russ smiled at her. "He's your collar. Go ahead and take him in while I make a few calls. I'll meet you inside."

He was letting her haul in Eustis to repair her reputation. Something he didn't need to do. But she was incredibly grateful nevertheless. Without thinking it through, she put her hand on his.

Surprise flashed across his face, but instead of pulling away, he gave her hand a quick squeeze and looked deep into her eyes. A quick shiver of awareness flared. She lost herself in the moment.

"It's gettin' hot back here," Eustis snapped from the back.

A shutter went down over Russ's eyes, and he released her hand.

Hissing out her emotions, she climbed out to retrieve Eustis. How had she so easily let Russ get to her? Was it because she saw the same longing for a relationship in his eyes as she knew filled her heart?

What difference did it make? He was not an option for so many reasons it wasn't even worth thinking about the possibility of a relationship with him.

She jerked Eustis from the backseat more forcefully than necessary, taking out her frustrations on the man. She needed to do a better job of focusing on the case. Not on Russ. She couldn't handle being hurt again as she had last year when her boyfriend bailed, saying he couldn't imagine a future that included Nikki. Her work and caring for Nikki would have to be enough right now, because Russ was totally off-limits.

EIGHT

Several hours after interrogating Eustis, Russ sat across a wide conference-room table from Sydney. Stolen-vehicle reports from Portland P.D. littered the table. Eustis admitted that the motorcycle in question had been in his possession, but he claimed he'd stolen it on a trip to the city a few weeks ago. DMV records didn't have a bike registered to Eustis, so they were inclined to believe him.

His other claim, that the bike had been stolen from the street outside Dixon's house while he sat in jail the night of Dixon's arrest, couldn't be verified as easily. Nor had they been able to confirm his alibi yet, so Eustis would remain in jail for the time being.

As Sydney focused on the reports, Russ used the time to study her. He couldn't help but smile at the memory of her interrogation of Eustis. She'd been strong. In control. Unflinching when Eustis tested her. The soft woman who'd tempted him in the car had been long gone.

His smile disappeared. He'd tried to suppress the feelings that had taken over his common sense so quickly, but they still lingered. He'd wanted to drop her hand in the car, lift his fingers to her face, smooth out the worry lines on her forehead and tell her everything would be okay. He didn't know what would've happened if Eustis hadn't been in the backseat.

Would he have followed through on his urge? Or would he have been able to do the right thing and resist like he had back in college? Did it even matter? Not hardly.

Sydney looked up and caught his staring. "What?"

"I was just thinking about how well you handled the questioning."

"I had good training. I watch *Law & Order* every week." She grinned, a sweet little smile that lit up her face.

He nodded at her hands. "So did you find anything in the reports?"

"Nothing yet." She stretched her arms behind her back and rolled her neck. "This is the part of detective work that's too boring to show on TV."

"Boring but necessary." He went back to looking at the papers before he let her distract him from their mission.

Eustis had given them the general location where he'd boosted the bike. Russ hoped to find the owner's name in these records. Since the bike was so expensive, the owner might've installed a GPS tracking device and it could lead them to their killer.

Russ's phone rang. "What's up, Garber?"

"A break in the case, that's what."

"I'm putting you on speaker so Deputy Tucker can hear this." Russ clicked the speaker button and set it between them on the table. "Go ahead, Garber."

"Baker just got back from talking to the parents of the girl who came in this morning."

"Rachelle," Russ said.

"Exactly. So the parents tell Baker she's an addict. They've tried everything to help her kick the habit but it hasn't worked because of the boyfriend. They get her clean and she goes back to the boyfriend, who is also her dealer."

"She dating Dixon?"

"Uh-uh. Your man Eustis."

Russ let the news settle over him and got a big smile on his face. "So if Eustis and Dixon were both dealing, maybe they were fighting for turf and Dixon lost the fight."

"Looks like it. Oh, and your search warrant for Eustis's place came through. I contacted the building manager. He's in apartment seven and will let you in."

Excitement over a real suspect filled the air.

"Good work, Garber. We'll head straight over there." By the time Russ ended the call, Sydney had moved to the door.

"Eager much?" he asked with a teasing tone.

"Are you kidding me? This could be the lead we were looking for. All we have to find is a gun or the phone he's been texting me on and this case is closed." She entered the hall at a quick clip.

They stepped into the brisk air. Russ kept his eyes alert. The killer could be hiding. Watching. Waiting to strike. One bullet was all it took. Despite Sydney's protest of being treated as less than an equal, he eased as close to her as he dared. They were moving too slow. She was at risk.

He laid a hand at the small of her back, urging her to move faster. He got a warning look from her, but he kept pushing until they reached the car. He opened her door. She cast him a stern reprimand with her eyes.

He didn't care. They'd made it this far...and he didn't intend to lose her.

And he kept the same viewpoint even though Sydney argued with him about it from the moment he climbed into the car until they reached the manager's door, where the burly man stood in an undershirt and torn jeans.

"I'm not climbing those stairs." The manager jerked his head at rusted metal stairs. "Here's the key. Bring it back when you're done." He slammed the door and bits of peeling paint slivered to the concrete.

"Nice." Russ held his hand out for Sydney to go before him.

Not liking this run-down complex, he surveyed the area and climbed the stairs next to Sydney, keeping his body between her and the parking lot. He switched sides on the landing until they found the apartment. If she noticed his protective actions, she didn't comment.

He opened the door. The stench of rotting garbage hit him in the face, but it was better than many of the odors he'd faced as a homicide detective.

Sydney held her hand over her mouth and nose and joined him in the combined living, dining and kitchen space. He gave the place a quick once-over. He would take pity on Sydney's sensitivity to the smell and let her stay by the door.

"You do this end of the room."

She moved closer to the door. "What would any girl see in this guy? I mean, this place is a pigsty." She shuddered. "And it's not like Eustis is so attractive or charming that she'd overlook all of this just to be with him."

He felt along the bottom of a table and pulled up a baggie of cocaine. "This is what she sees in him."

"But if what her parents said is true, she's been clean and still comes back. She has to get a good look at him and this place when she's sober."

"The craving for the drug is so strong she doesn't care." His struggle to overcome his addiction to alcohol rang through in his tone. He regretted saying anything the moment the words left his mouth.

Looking up, Sydney peered at him for a few long moments. Searching. Testing. Her eyes seemed to pierce through to his soul before he looked away.

"Sounds like you're speaking from personal experience," she said.

He had the urge to blurt out his past, but couldn't stand to think of how she'd react. "Something like that."

"Something like that, or you've had firsthand experience?"

He glanced at her. Saw only caring, not judgment, so he shared a little more. "Alcohol, not drugs."

"Someone close to you." Her eyes were so soft, warm. Encouraging him to get to know her better by sharing his life with her.

And he wanted to respond. To tell her about his past. To see if she could look beyond his failings to see the man he was today. But he had to stop thinking that way. He couldn't involve her in his mess of a life. It would do neither of them any good if he told her about his past.

"You find anything yet?"

Flashing a look of disappointment at him, she shook her head.

He jerked out another drawer, slid his fingers under papers and along the sides. Nothing. Frustration started to bubble up.

"I found a laptop." Her voice rang with the thrill of discovery. "I'm gonna boot it up to see what we have."

She pulled a silver notebook computer out from under the sofa and sat. She opened it and he went back to searching. He systematically made his way around the space, finding nothing of interest.

"Jackpot," she cried out. "I think this is Dixon's missing computer. Did you notice the brand on the power cord you found at his house?"

"Sony."

"Then change that from *I think* to *I'm almost positive*." She looked up, her eyes burning with excitement. "The question is why did Eustis have Dixon's laptop?"

"I'm finished here. Let's take it back to the office and check it out."

They closed up the apartment and returned the key to the manager. In the car, Sydney opened the laptop again and clicked on keys. He didn't know if she was so intent on searching the computer to find a lead or if she was hurt because he'd clammed up earlier. Either way, they made the ride back to the sheriff's office in silence.

Just as well. It allowed him to focus on their surroundings and make sure no one followed.

As they pulled into the lot, his cell rang. He checked caller ID. Garber. "What's up?"

"There's been an assault at 113 State Street," the officer said.

Russ's gut tightened. That was Sydney's street.

"Hold on." Russ clamped his hand over the mouthpiece. "Isn't 113 State Street the other side of your duplex?"

"Yeah, my friend Kate Cleary lives there, why?"

"Dispatch just reported an assault at that address." Her face paled. "Someone hurt Kate?"

"Looks like it."

Russ resumed his conversation with Garber, confirming his officer was en route to the scene before disconnecting and looking at Sydney. He could almost see her thoughts racing through her head.

"This is because of me, isn't it?" she choked out.

"Not because of you, but this's probably related to Dixon's murder."

"I need to go see if Kate's okay," she insisted.

"I wouldn't advise that. This could be a setup to bring you into the line of fire."

"I don't care what it is." Fierce determination filled her voice. "Kate is my friend. I'm going. If you won't drive me, I'll get one of the guys here to take me." Their eyes met. A dance of wills ensued.

"I'll take you under one condition," he said, letting her know by his tone that he wasn't doing so willingly.

"Name it."

"You will listen and follow every directive I give you at the scene."

"Fine," she reluctantly agreed.

"Fine or yes, Russ, I promise to listen to you?"

"I promise."

"Then let's go." He pulled back onto the road and they drove in silence.

His phone rang, startling both of them. He answered the call, listening intently as Garber explained what happened at the duplex.

"Good work," he responded. "I'm three minutes out. Establish a perimeter, clear the house and don't touch anything until I get there." He clicked off his phone. "Garber's at the scene. Your neighbor will be fine. Looks like a head wound. Maybe a concussion. She's already on the way to the hospital."

Sydney sighed out a shaky breath. "Did he say what happened?"

"She heard a commotion in your half of the duplex and checked it out. There was an intruder. He plowed her down as he took off."

Her eyes widened. "Someone broke into my place?"

"That's what your friend said."

"What's going on?" Her tone soured with frustration.

"I think it's pretty obvious. Our killer decided to move forward and search your house for the item he wants."

As he watched fear consume her face, the air between them seemed to evaporate. He wanted to pull her into his arms, promise that he'd take care of her and keep her from harm. But they were driving down a busy street, nosy people all around them. And thank goodness they were. Otherwise, he might forget all the reasons he shouldn't follow through on his feelings when his focus should be on finding the man who still threatened her.

* * *

As they turned onto her street, Sydney's hands shook with rage over someone hurting her friend. She was so shaken up she didn't even bother to tell Russ to back off with the Mr. Protective mode. Instead, she wanted to scream out her frustration over what happened to Kate.

Though Kate was already on the way to the hospital, a vision of her wheelchair tipped on its side and Kate lying on the ground, bleeding and confused, flashed into Sydney's head. Sweet, dependable Kate didn't deserve this. She'd already faced enough challenges with the onset of multiple sclerosis a few years ago and then losing her ability to walk last year. Sydney couldn't imagine being confined to a wheelchair, but Kate took it all in stride, saying God could use her in a chair as much as he could use her on her feet.

Sydney wished her faith was that strong. Here she'd been blubbering like a baby over what had been happening in her life and Kate was probably trying to help those who came to her rescue. She was too special to involve in this mess.

Sydney bowed her head. *Lord, please hold Kate in Your arms,* she prayed. *Heal her wounds. Help us to find the person terrorizing all of us and bring him to justice.*

Feeling a bit better, Sydney raised her head and waited for the first glimpse of her second crime scene in less than twenty-four hours. She wanted to look away but she couldn't.

There it was. What she'd dreaded. Kate's wheelchair, frame bent, lying at the base of concrete steps that abutted a ramp. A large bloodstain had soaked into the concrete. She was lucky to be alive and Sydney was lucky to still have her friend.

Russ turned off the car then laid a hand on her arm. "Are you sure you're ready to see this?"

She nearly laughed, perhaps in hysteria. "I saw a man murdered last night. How could a burglary be worse?"

He caught and held her gaze. "This is a personal attack, Syd. Someone violated your space."

He was right, but she couldn't cower in the car. She had to see what the intruder had done. Shaking off Russ's hand, she jumped out of the vehicle and pressed her way through the neighbors who tossed out questions she ignored. She took the steps to her front door two at a time.

Russ was hot on her heels as he moved his way through the group with sharp *excuse mes*. When she reached the landing, she heard him call out for her to wait up, but she ignored him.

At the door standing ajar, she took a few calming breaths then peered into her family room.

She gasped, then felt her throat constrict.

The sofa lay overturned with the fabric slashed open. The cushions had suffered the same fate. Items she'd collected over the years lay shattered in tiny fragments on the hardwood floor. Instead of shaking with fright as she had expected, her anger flared to the surface. This was the last straw. She wouldn't let this creep get away with invasion of her privacy.

She knew Garber had cleared the house, so she entered the family room. Careful not to disturb the crime scene, she picked her way through the mess room by room. Kitchen, bathroom, both bedrooms. All trashed in the same way. Everything she owned had been touched by this assailant.

What kind of person did something like this?

She dropped onto a hard kitchen chair, the jolt adding to her misery. Frustration and fatigue replaced the anger. Her cell chimed from her pocket. Hoping it was news about Kate, Sydney pulled it out.

The same number from last night.

Her heart started racing. She looked up to catch Russ's gaze.

He came up behind her as she thumbed the buttons to read the message.

Welcome home, Deputy Tucker. Sorry I left such a mess, but I will find what I'm looking for. When I do, your life will end.

She felt the blood drain from her face.

She still had no clue what item the text referred to, but the perpetrator had made his point very clear.

He'd assaulted her friend and trashed her house in his desperate quest for this thing…and was willing to kill again once he found it.

NINE

This situation was out of control. Russ wanted to do something—anything—to protect Sydney from the danger. All color had drained from her face. She sat silently on the chair, staring at her cell phone. The message clearly terrified her, but like last night, he was equally concerned that the killer had to be watching them. Perhaps in the group of locals outside. Russ didn't want to alarm her, but he needed to check it out.

"I need to talk with Garber," he said then gave her a quick smile to try to ease her concern.

"I'll go with you."

"It's safer for you to stay inside." He turned away, working hard with each step to push her tormented face out of his mind.

On the porch, he surveyed the scene. The group of onlookers had grown. He counted twenty anxious faces peering up at the house. Garber held a notepad in his hand and talked with the bystanders.

Garber followed protocol, taking down names and

asking what they'd seen. It was common practice for a criminal to hang in a group of looky-loos to admire the chaos their actions had caused. If their killer was out there, Russ wanted to record it. He pulled out his cell and snapped a few pictures.

Certain he'd gotten a clear shot of each person, Russ went to join Garber.

"A word," Russ said and moved out of earshot of the crowd. "I believe our killer is tailing Deputy Tucker. Take extra care in recording everyone's name. Keep your eyes open. Detain anyone acting suspicious."

Garber eyed Russ. "This isn't like you. What's got you so spooked?"

Russ didn't like that he'd not controlled his concern for Sydney. He needed to play it cooler. He didn't want to start any rumors. Though Garber was a sharp cookie and might see right through it, Russ's best bet now was to redirect the conversation. "Why don't you bring me up to speed on what happened so far and we'll go from there."

Garber spent a few seconds studying Russ, but then shrugged it off. "Didn't have long to talk to the victim before transport. She claims the incident occurred a few hours ago. She laid there waiting for someone to find her. Intruder wore a ski mask so she couldn't ID him. Said he was tall, but coming from someone in a wheelchair, her perspective may be skewed."

"That all?" Russ let his irritation flow through his words.

"Like I said, I didn't have long to talk to her."

Russ bristled at Garber's testy tone, but he deserved his officer's attitude. He'd let his worry for Sydney make Garber feel incompetent. No good would come from demoralizing his staff. He needed to make amends.

He clapped Garber's back. "Sorry. I was hoping we'd get a break in this case by now and I took it out on you."

"So Eustis's place was a bust?"

"Not completely." Russ told him about the computer. "We also received another text. With Eustis in jail, it pretty much rules him out as our killer."

"Maybe there's something on the computer."

"I'll check it out as soon as possible. When you get back to the office, see if Eustis will explain why the computer was in his possession."

Garber grinned. "It will be my pleasure to lean on the creep."

"As always, keep me in the loop about any new developments," Russ said and headed for the house.

On the way, a sense of unease sent chills up his back. He spun and searched the crowd, but nothing had changed. He let his search widen to the surrounding area. He saw nothing, but the killer could still be hiding...watching.

He shook off the feeling and went inside. He found Sydney picking through the rubble on the family-room floor.

"You okay?" he asked, making sure to keep all emotion out of his tone.

"I'm fine."

He didn't miss her censuring tone or the look that said "here we are again, you're treating me like a damsel in distress in front of my fellow officers." But how could he not when the strain of the events hung in her eyes and a renewed drive to protect her kept his mind divided between the job and her pain?

He remembered what a training officer had taught him to get through a victim's grief when it became overwhelming—look away from their face until he could control his emotions. That should work. For now, anyway.

He focused on the trashed room. "Anything missing?"

"Not that I can tell. Our electronics are all here, so I assume the intruder was looking for the item in the text message."

"You check the phone number for the text?"

"Same one as last night."

"Not that I ever liked Eustis for the murder, but this at least proves he's not behind the threatening texts. He couldn't have sent this text from jail."

"But he could still be involved somehow," she reminded him. "Especially since he had Dixon's computer. We need to look at it as soon as we can."

"We'll get started on that as soon as we finish processing this scene. If we're lucky, the cell-phone registration will have panned out by then and we'll also have an address to check out."

The sudden fear in her eyes opened a clear window into her inner turmoil. They'd eventually learn if the registration for the cell was bogus, but would they do so before the killer returned and would she live long enough for it to make a difference?

Russ led the way down the long corridor to Kate's hospital room. He hadn't wanted to take Sydney to such a public place, but after what she'd gone through, he couldn't say no when she'd asked to stop by and make sure her friend was okay.

The drive over had been uneventful, even more so than he'd expected. No matter what subject he raised, he hadn't elicited more than one-word answers from Sydney.

Until he mentioned moving her and Nikki to a safe house. Then she'd blown up and said as a police officer, she could take care of herself. He never wanted to hear that comment again, but he had to admit he was treating her differently than his men. But then, their eyes didn't make him want to fix all of their problems and give them a life they deserved.

The same eyes that, as they now approached Kate's hospital room, overflowed with pain for her injured friend.

He stepped in front of her just outside the door. "I realize Kate's your friend and you want some time to be alone with her, but Garber had little time to question her. I'd like to talk to her first. Then I'll leave the two of you alone."

"Agreed, but I'll be present during the questioning."

That was too easy. He'd expected an argument. Might still get one. "I'll do all the talking."

She opened her mouth to speak but he held up his hand. "The minute you lay eyes on Kate, you'll want to protect her. Some of my questions might upset her. You'll want to answer for her or jump to her defense. I can't have you doing either one."

"Is giving her a hug out of the question?" Her sarcasm should have made him mad, but after the sullen ride here, he liked seeing her spunk return.

"A hug is perfectly acceptable behavior." He smiled and could see she was disappointed that he didn't rise to her bait. He held out his hand and hung back. "After you."

She raced across the room to her friend and pulled her into her arms. The pair didn't exchange any words, but they seemed very close, something he was definitely missing in his life. Something that after time spent with Sydney seemed more important.

Sure, he had two brothers, both of whom would come to his aid when he asked, but since he'd disappointed everyone with his dive into alcohol, he wanted to stand on his own and prove he'd regained control of his life. So he'd gotten prickly about accepting help and they'd learned to wait until he requested their assistance.

"Enough," Kate said, extricating herself from Sydney's arms.

"You sure you're okay?" Sydney perched on the side of the bed.

"Fine." Kate peered around Sydney. "I'd recognize you anywhere, Chief Morgan." She gave him a flirtatious wink then held out her hand. "Kate Cleary."

He ignored the reaction he sometimes got from women and shook her hand. "Wish we could've met under different circumstances."

"Me, too, but then sometimes God likes to toss a few surprises into our lives to get our attention. I wake up each day waiting to see what He'll do next."

Russ believed in God, but wasn't sure how to respond to this enthusiastic expression of faith. "Mind if I ask you a few questions about the incident?"

She grinned with the innocence of a child. "Avoiding the subject of God, I see."

"Not avoiding entirely. Just sidestepping for now." He glanced at Sydney, who seemed to enjoy his discomfort.

"Fair enough," Kate said. "What did you want to know?"

"Tell me what happened."

"Not much to tell. It all happened so fast." She faced Sydney. "I heard a noise next door. Thought maybe Nikki decided to skip school. I wanted to encourage her to go back before she gave you something else to worry about."

Sydney patted her friend's hand. "Thank you for looking out for me."

"But it wasn't Nikki," Russ said to get her back on track.

"No." She shuddered. "I pounded on the door and yelled for Nikki. The door flew open. A man rushed out and shoved me out of the way. My chair caught on a column and crashed down the stairs. I laid there until Mrs. Jaxon came home and called 911." She sighed. "And that's all I can tell you."

Sydney's face constricted in pain and regret.

"Can you describe the man?" Russ asked before Sydney could waylay the conversation by expressing her sorrow over what happened.

"Not his face. He wore one of those black ski masks. He was tall, though." She studied Russ. "Taller than you. Not muscular, but thin. Wiry."

"What was he wearing?"

"Jeans. A black leather biker's jacket. Black leather boots."

"What else did you see while you were lying there?"

"Nothing, really. I was facing the house and my legs were wedged in so I couldn't scoot around."

"Maybe you heard or even smelled something that could help."

"Maybe." She stared off into the distance. "There

was one thing, but I don't see how it could be related."

"Why don't you tell me? I'll decide if it's important." Russ ended with a smile meant to encourage Kate to talk.

She smiled back. "Shortly after I fell, a motorcycle roared down the alley,"

Russ locked gazes with Sydney. Saw the same conclusion in her eyes.

Kate looked from one to the other and back again. "What're you two not telling me?"

"It's really nothing." Russ worked to keep his tone laid-back. "Did you hear anything else?"

"I don't think so, but give me a second to think about it." Kate closed her eyes.

Sydney's cell chimed. Russ watched her click to the text and gawk at the message. She glanced at Kate, then motioned for him to come closer.

He bent over the phone.

Nice of you to visit your friend, Deputy Tucker. If you keep stonewalling me, you'll make another trip to the hospital. But then you'll visit the morgue.

Russ's protective instincts shot to attention. He went to the window and let his gaze sweep the area below. Seeing nothing out of the ordinary, he drew the blinds.

Kate opened her eyes. "Other than birds and dogs, that's— What's wrong?"

Sydney palmed her cell and forced out a laugh. "Nothing. Everything will be fine."

Russ forced back his concern and smiled. "Sydney's right. Everything will be fine."

His tone was calm, soothing even, but he could see that he didn't fool Sydney. She knew this killer had to be smart and cunning to know her exact location right now.

Russ needed to step up his plans. Quickly.

"That's all for now." He handed his business card to Kate. "If you think of anything else, call my cell." He turned to Sydney. "I'll wait outside for you."

"I won't keep her long." Kate smiled a sincere goodbye to Russ.

Sydney and Russ exchanged a long, knowing look as he walked to the door. She drew in a quick breath, then put on a brave smile that she aimed at Kate as he left the room.

With his staff already stretched to the breaking point, he found a secluded spot in a waiting area off the busy hallway and called county for a protective detail. He could be overreacting, but experience from tracking down many killers said their suspect knew what he was doing. If they left Kate unprotected, he'd strike.

Next, he dialed his older brother, Reid. As an ex-FBI agent, he had skills no one else in the area possessed. Russ dreaded asking for more help from the guy who'd single-handedly pulled Russ out of the pit of his alcoholic binge—he'd done enough for Russ—but lives were at stake and he needed the best on his team.

"Hey, bro," Russ said after Reid answered. "I hate to do this, but I need a favor."

"I'm listening." Reid's cautious tone was courtesy of his years as a fed.

"You remember Sydney Tucker?" Russ asked even though he was sure Reid knew her. Last year Reid's daughter, Jessie, had been abducted and Nikki had helped keep her safe until she was rescued.

"Nikki's older sister, right?"

"Right. So she's a deputy now and someone is trying to kill her." Russ recounted the events of the past two days. "I was hoping you'd let her, along with Nikki and their neighbor, stay at Valley View." Valley View was the family resort Reid had come home to manage after his wife, Diane, died so he was more available for his daughter.

"They can stay at the lodge. It's the easiest building to secure."

"Great…thanks. We need to get Nikki from school. She's out at three. An hour or so for the traffic to clear. Then we'll be there."

"I'll arrange for a sitter for Jessie and head over to the lodge."

"Thanks, Reid. Keep your eyes and ears open."

Reid chuckled. "OPSEC advice from my little brother. How touching." OPSEC—operations security—was one of Reid's areas of expertise.

"Okay, fine. You don't need me to tell you what to do, but still be careful."

"This guy's really got you freaked." His tone had sobered.

"Totally. He isn't tailing us, but somehow he's figured out our every move. Until I know how he's doing it, I have to overreact." Russ disconnected and headed for the cafeteria.

They hadn't eaten since early morning. If they were going to stay ahead of this cunning foe, they needed to keep up their strength. After he dropped off the meal with Sydney, he'd head over to the hospital administrator's office to solicit his help in transporting Sydney to Valley View.

Once the arrangements were in place, all Russ had to do was convince Sydney to go along with him.

He could already see her jaw jutting out at a stubborn angle. Her arms crossed as he explained the details. Maybe a flash of independence as she declared she was strong enough to care for herself. No doubt about it—he had a tough job ahead of him.

He let out a tired sigh.

How would he ever convince a woman who fought so hard for her independence to follow his directives so that they could keep her safe and catch the killer?

TEN

Sydney sat on the edge of Kate's bed, clasping her hand as she offered thanks to the Lord for keeping both of them safe and petitioned for quick closure to this mess. They sat together, the peace of God surrounding them, but Sydney's heart still felt heavy.

Why couldn't she trust God and let go of this worry?

Perhaps if this maniac was only gunning for her, she could. But he'd crossed the line and included Nikki and Kate, so the fear remained firmly lodged.

After a squeeze of Kate's hand, Sydney opened her eyes. "I'm really sorry this happened, Kate. Your chair is pretty much toast. When we get back to the station, I'll arrange to have a new one delivered."

Kate arched a brow, directing Sydney's eyes to the wide bandage circling her friend's head. "Don't do this, Syd."

"Do what?"

"You're focusing on the one thing in this mess that

makes me different from everyone else." She sighed. "If this criminal ran over another friend, what would you be doing?"

"I'd hold their hand and tell them everything will be all right."

Kate held out her hand. "So be my friend and let me take care of the wheelchair."

"Okay, friend." Sydney smiled back. Not a forced smile this time, but a genuine show of affection for the woman who'd overcome so much. Part of that strength came from not highlighting her differences, but from letting people see Kate the person, not Kate the handicapped woman.

"So as my friend, why don't you tell me what's really going on." Kate held up her free hand. "And before you protest, I'm not blind. I saw the looks you shared with Chief Morgan when he was in here."

"It's nothing for you to worry about."

"Ha! Like I believe that. I got a good look in your family room before I hit the ground. I'm not a cop, but I've watched enough cop shows on TV to know that wasn't a simple burglary." A shadow crossed her face. "Someone was looking for something, and I'm worried about you and Nikki."

"You don't need to worry about us. We're safe."

She gave an irritated sigh. "I don't believe you, Syd, and I won't quit asking questions until you tell me the whole story."

She was asking for privileged information—something Sydney couldn't give. "I can't, Kate. Russ's in charge of this investigation, and I can't give out details without his permission."

"Russ, is it?" Her eyes lit with renewed interest. "I didn't know you were on a first-name basis."

Sydney had blown it again. This was exactly the image she didn't want to put into the ever-impetuous Kate's mind. Or anyone else's, for that matter. She needed to be careful in the future to use Russ's title, especially around other officers.

At least her little slipup had taken her friend's mind off the other issue. "Don't read anything into this, Kate. It's pretty hard to change what you call a guy you've known for years."

Kate studied Sydney's face, which grew hot under the scrutiny. "You're not telling me everything again. Something else is going on here, too, isn't there?"

"You are the most frustrating friend in all the universe. Always trying to dig up something that doesn't exist."

"I'm not digging up anything. Your face tells it all. Besides worry about the break-in there's a healthy dose of respect for Chief Morgan, along with something else sparking in your eye. I think you're developing a thing for our good chief." Kate smiled softly. "I don't like the circumstances, but, oh, how I hope something does develop between you two."

Sydney shook her head. "You of all people know men are off-limits until after Nikki is out on her own."

"Ah, but that doesn't mean you're not interested, does it?"

Sydney let go of Kate's hand. "What I want is for you to get some rest."

"The only way that'll happen is if you get your Russ in here and make him tell me what's happening."

"He's not my Russ," she insisted.

"Fine, but I'm serious about wanting to talk to him. Will you please ask him to come back?"

"If you promise to drop this whole matchmaking thing."

"Deal."

"Okay, then." She squeezed Kate's hand and went to find Russ.

In the corridor, she stopped short before running into fellow deputy Tom Young. His arms were crossed over a massive chest, his eyes tight with concern.

"What're you doing here?" she asked him.

"Morgan requested a protection detail for your friend."

She was surprised Russ asked for county help, but he'd probably stretched his staff as far as he could. "Where is the chief?"

Young pointed down the hall to where Russ stood near a nurses' station talking with a white-coated doctor. They had to be discussing Kate, and she didn't like the grim expression on the doctor's face.

Kate's MS could complicate things. Something more serious could be wrong.

Anxious for an update, she headed toward the two men. On the way across the corridor, she thumbed through calls she'd missed while praying with Kate. She pulled up a text from Nikki.

Who knew having a bodyguard could make you a rock star. :)

Happy over the jubilant tone to the message, Sydney lightened up a bit. If only her sister could keep her spirits up until this horrible situation ended. She just prayed it ended without anyone else getting hurt.

As she moved forward, she continued to watch Russ, memorizing his sparse movements. The doctor gestured wildly, but Russ held firm, like a strong tree that could withstand great gusts of wind. As if feeling her eyes on him, he looked up. His eyes telegraphed the same strength.

Though he seemed to keep his emotions battened down due to something in his past, he'd proven that he was a man to count on. A man who would do his best to protect anyone who needed him. A man—if she ever forgot that men were capable of abandoning those they claimed to love—that she could see getting to know better. But men did bail when the going got tough. For all she knew, Russ was just like her father, or the other guys who'd taken off when they'd learned of her responsibility to Nikki.

Before she reached them, Russ shook hands with the doctor, then came down the hallway and nodded for her to follow him.

He stopped near the emergency-exit door. "That's Kate's doctor. He confirmed this overnight stay is only precautionary because of her other health issues and expects to release her tomorrow."

Tears of joy rushed out. As hard as she tried to stop them, they slipped down her cheeks.

She swiped a hand at her eyes. "You must really think I'm a total failure as a police officer."

"Why...because you cry?"

She nodded. "At least with your staff, you never have to deal with this."

"That's true. Instead I deal with what happens when they keep things bottled up."

"If it was just me, I could deal. But when he threatened Kate, I couldn't—" Her voice broke.

"It's really okay to cry, Syd. After you've worked in law enforcement long enough, you realize one of the hardest things we face is seeing bad things happen to good people. It's harder when it happens to someone you care about." His eyes softened. "It's even worse when we feel responsible for what's happening."

She let herself linger on his eyes. Then she saw the pain he'd buried rise to the surface and sit on his face like a weeping sore. She reached out, rubbed his upper arm. As soon as she touched him, the hard shell closed over like plated armor, and he looked away.

She removed her hand, but she wouldn't forget what she'd seen. He was too good of a man to live with this pain. She hoped somehow to repay him for risking his life to keep her and those she loved safe. Maybe she could do that by helping him work through whatever this issue was so he could take back his life.

Russ tamped down the urge to tell Sydney what had happened to Willie Babcock and how it had sent him down the spiral of self-destruction. He knew how she was feeling.

Helpless, angry, confused.

All melded together in a rage that could consume her if she let it. But he wouldn't let that happen to her.

If he stayed strong, she'd have someone to rely on and keep her from feeling the sheer despair and hopelessness he'd felt. As vulnerable as she was right now, he'd redirect her focus by sharing his plan.

He sought her eyes again. The compassion and caring nearly pulled him back into that place he avoided, but he shook it off.

"I haven't figured out how the killer knew you were here, but however he did it, we have to step up security." He saw disappointment at the change of subject, but so be it. "We've swept this wing and posted a protective detail for Kate."

"What happens tomorrow? She obviously can't go home."

"I've arranged a safe house for you and Nikki for tonight. Kate can join you tomorrow."

"No. Just take Nikki and Kate. The further they are away from me the better."

"And what about you? The killer isn't about to stop until he gets what he wants from you. I can't let you put yourself in danger." He took a defensive stance and trained his eyes on her.

"They're better off without me."

"You really think it will be better for Nikki in a strange place without her big sister there to keep her from worrying?" The narrowing of her eyes said he'd hit a nerve so he continued. "Commit to one day. Just one, Syd. Then we'll reevaluate if needed."

"Fine. But I won't be left out of the investigation."

"I'll be half of the protection detail, so you'll know what's going on the minute I do."

He waited for her to balk at the fact that he was part of her detail, but she gave a clipped nod and said, "Now we need to see Kate. The only way she'd agree to your plan is if she knows what's going on." She sighed. "I hate that we have to scare her like this, but I know how strong-willed she is. This is the only way she'll cooperate."

He wanted to chuckle. Sydney could see the

stubborn streaks in Nikki and Kate, but she didn't have a clue she possessed the trait herself. This tenacity drew him like a magnet and he wanted to spend time with her. To get to know her better.

Focus on the work, Russ.

"I'll break it to Kate," he said. "You can stay out here."

She shook her head. "I won't let Kate go through this alone."

"Then let's do this." He didn't wait for her to agree, but strode toward Kate's room. She might be lying in a bed from being attacked and confined to a wheelchair from MS, but she was a rich woman for having a strong protector like Sydney.

He pushed open Kate's door and let Sydney enter before him. She crossed the room, sat on the side of the bed and placed a protective arm around Kate's back. Her face reminded him of a fierce mother cat protecting her kittens from an attacker.

It left him feeling lonely, isolated.

He loved his job and Zack was in his life again. Maybe he didn't see him as often as he wanted, but as much as was possible after how he'd treated his family. He'd thought his life was good, but his time with Sydney made him want to let down his guard for once and find someone who cared about him as she did her family.

He fisted his hands and joined the women.

No use in wishing for things that never could be. He'd ruined his chance at that kind of life. It'd be so much easier if he kept his focus on reality. He had a great job that he loved, a son he saw on weekends, and that would have to be enough.

With the final transport details nailed down, Russ knocked softly on Kate's door before pushing it open. Kate slept and Sydney sat on a hard chair by the bed, her face peaceful as she gazed at her friend. A surprise to be sure.

She looked up at him and smiled.

How could she have achieved such calm? An hour or so ago when he'd left her with Kate, she'd been tense and overwhelmed. Now this?

"We're ready to go," he whispered so as not to wake Kate.

He held open the door and she joined him in the hallway.

"I've been thinking." She paused.

He prepared for the inevitable argument by fisting his hands.

"We need to reconsider not housing me with Nikki and Kate."

"This isn't up for discussion, Syd."

"Please hear me out." She laid a hand on his arm, the warmth of her fingers threatening to thaw his resolve. "I can stay at home. This guy won't try to kill me. He thinks I have something he wants and if he kills me, he'll never get it. But if he goes after me, maybe abducts Kate or Nikki, then he has the leverage he needs to force me to talk." She sighed heavily. "Since I have nothing to give him, he'd kill them to prove a point. I can't let that happen."

"You have a valid concern, but if you don't lie low, he'll snatch you and try to make you talk."

"At least I won't lead him to Kate and Nikki."

Russ leaned back and looked at Sydney. She was arguing with him, but all emotion was absent from her voice and her body language. Almost as if she'd made some sort of decision and she was at peace. Maybe she'd decided she had to die to let Nikki and Kate live.

Well, he wouldn't have any part of that. "You already agreed to this plan."

"I know, but only for one night. Can't we move them to another location tomorrow?"

"Maybe. I'll have Reid check with his friends at the Bureau to see if he can secure another safe house. Somewhere out of the area. Does that work for you?"

Her beaming smile was more than answer enough.

"Then let's get this show on the road. First stop is the school to pick up Nikki."

"That could lead the killer right to her."

"As smart as this guy is, he already knows where Nikki goes to school. Besides, I have a plan to ensure he can't follow us." Hoping he could accomplish what he'd promised, he jerked his head in the direction they needed to go. "This way. Stay close."

She followed him without question to the service

elevator. He hoped her willingness to comply meant she trusted him, not that she'd given up and would bail somewhere along the way. He'd rather think she'd based her compliance on trust. Liked the idea that she might trust him. It had been a long time since he'd felt anyone relied on him other than his officers.

From the elevator car, he led her down into the bowels of the hospital until they reached a large storage room.

"I didn't want to take a chance that we were made in my cruiser," he said. "So we'll be transported in a delivery truck. You okay with that?"

"Fine." Another one-word answer.

Had all of the fight gone out of her? She didn't appear defeated, just calm. Serene, even.

What was going on with her?

She'd had the same easy peace early this morning, too, but had lost it when Kate got hurt. Now it was back and it was so foreign to this spunky woman that it worried him.

He continued through the room to the loading dock, where a delivery truck had backed in. "One of my men will drive us. To determine if we're being followed, he'll make a few stops on the normal delivery route." He pointed into the truck. "All the way to the front."

He followed her between stacks of boxes to a cleared section. "Have a seat."

When she'd settled on a pile of furniture pads, he

secured cargo netting to metal tines and his officer stacked boxes to create a wall.

He sat opposite her. "Once they finish loading we'll be out of here."

"Thanks for arranging this." She smiled softly. "I'm sorry for all the extra work I've caused by insisting on coming to see Kate."

"No problem." He returned her smile and she settled against the wall.

Her easygoing mood should have made him relax, but as his officer stacked boxes to the ceiling, the light in their small cave grew dimmer and the reality of their situation kept him on edge.

"Do you think all of this is really necessary?" she asked.

He peered at her to see if fear had usurped her calm, but he couldn't make out her eyes in the dim light. "I'm pretty sure the killer didn't make us in my cruiser, but even if he didn't, he could assume that we'd move you out of here that way."

"Or he could think you'd do it another way and watch all traffic out of the hospital."

"That's why we have two trucks leaving at the same time," he replied. "He only has a fifty-fifty chance of tailing the right one. When we stop for deliveries, we'll know if he's followed us.

His radio squawked. "That's it, Chief. We're closing the doors now. See you on the other side."

Russ acknowledged the call. Once they were moving, he retrieved his flashlight from his duty belt, turned it on and strapped it facing up in a cord on the wall. The light reflected off the ceiling, bouncing softly down on Sydney. Eyes closed, she'd laid her hands palm-up on her knees, as if settling into a meditative trance.

While her eyes were closed, he had no qualms about openly studying her. Her facial muscles were relaxed. Her lips moved silently. She seemed to be praying, and he was beginning to see she lived her faith in a much more intense way than he did.

He hadn't been raised in a Christian household, but when his life fell apart, his brothers, who'd found Christ through their own turmoil, helped him see the need for God. In fact, faith had brought him back from the brink of self-destruction. He owed God big-time for that.

But then what happened? The divorce. Losing custody of Zack. He'd let his faith slide away with it. Not consciously. He'd just stopped making it a priority. Hadn't really even noticed the loss until now. Maybe he should take a hint from Sydney and ask for a little guidance here. He certainly wasn't handling things too well alone.

"First stop." His officer's voice startled him.

Now wasn't the time for prayer or small talk with Sydney. As the truck slowed, Russ turned off the light, then clamped a hand on his gun and listened. The back door opened, boxes shifted, then the door closed again.

He let out the breath he'd been holding and waited

in the darkness. He could hear Sydney moving around. He wondered what she was thinking. Her foot settled against his calf. He expected her to jerk it away, but she must not have realized it was touching him. He liked the connection. Liked knowing she was safe next to him.

The truck started moving again. He flipped on the light. It took a few seconds for his eyes to adjust, but when they did he found Sydney peering at him.

"You said back at the hospital that the hardest part of this job is seeing bad things happen to good people."

"Yeah."

"I'm not sure I agree," she said.

"Then what?

"I think it's when the people who do bad things get away with it." She crossed her arms. "I mean, when bad things happen to us, we can use it to grow and become better people. But when these creeps get away with something, it encourages them to do it again."

"But is it fair for a good person to have to go through the agony and pain?"

"Fair? No." She paused, seemed to ponder her next words. "But take what's going on now. Once all of this's over, I can use what I've learned on the job to help someone else."

"That's a pretty noble goal, but is it realistic? In my experience, we spend more time focusing on the perpetrators than on helping others."

"We do, but if we touch one person, isn't everything else worth it?"

"I'll have to think about that."

"What's to think about?" She sat forward. "I'm a perfect example, with what Vicki did for Nikki and me."

He found her dream to help others admirable but wondered how long it would be before she gave up on that plan. He'd seen other officers go the extra mile like this, but they'd often burned out or were taken advantage of, so they gave up their quest.

The truck slowed for their next stop. He studied her face, which was beaming with hope for a better tomorrow. Maybe she'd be an exception, like the officer who'd helped her. But in order for her to succeed, he had to protect her from a killer who'd proven his prowess.

ELEVEN

Sydney could tell Russ thought her desire to help others was naïve. Not surprising. At the academy, others had scoffed at what they'd called her unrealistic viewpoint, but she knew for a fact that she could combine her faith and her career to achieve a positive influence in others' lives.

She'd always thought the influence would be on someone in the community, but maybe God had put her in this situation to help Russ with whatever anguish he seemed to be facing. His family hadn't been church-going folks, but she'd seen his brothers at church, so maybe Russ had become a Christian, too. When the door closed again, she'd broach the subject.

But how did she start? Maybe she could tell him how her faith had helped her in the past. She hadn't been a good example for him, though. Actions spoke louder than words. She'd let these events toss her around like a tiny boat in a storm. He might not believe anything she told him. She'd have to tread lightly.

At the click of the door, the light evaporated. She could hear Russ fumbling for his flashlight in the dark. This was the perfect opportunity to speak without worrying about any nonverbal cues he threw her way.

"I wanted to thank you for being so understanding during this mess." She took a deep breath and rushed on before he could try to change the subject. "Seems to me the only way you could empathize so well is if you've been involved in a similar situation."

"Yeah." His tone was flat, devoid of all emotions.

"So someone died and you thought you should've been able to save them?"

"Yeah."

She heard him tapping his light against his palm. "Do you want to talk about it?"

"No."

"Sometimes talking helps."

"Talked to the shrink the department insisted I see. Didn't stop the nightmares or regret. So I'm done talking." The finality in his tone made her want to stop but the darkness gave her courage to continue.

"I don't know if you believe in God, but He also listens."

"Tried that, too."

She'd offer an open-ended question so he wouldn't shut her down again. "And?"

"He was there to bring me through the worst of it, but now I'm on my own." His tone was thick with despair. "You mind turning on your Maglite. Mine's dead."

She reached for her flashlight and took this as his way of saying he'd closed the conversation. But as far as she was concerned, it wasn't over. Maybe for now, but not forever. The ache in his voice ensured that she'd continue trying to get him to open up and share what was eating away at him.

For now, she settled back and rode in silence as the truck made a few more stops before the final one at the school. In a dimly-lit garage the size of a large barn, Russ exited the truck and she followed. Nikki was seated at a card table on the far side of the room, playing cards with her bodyguard.

She looked up, spotted Sydney and raced across the large space. "What's going on? No one around here will tell me anything."

Sydney moved her sister into a secluded section of the room. Careful to keep her voice calm, she described the trashing of their duplex.

"Are you kidding me? Someone busted into our place?" Nikki's eyes welled. "Did they take my computer? Or iPod? Please tell me they didn't take that."

"It wasn't a burglary. I got another text message. This guy is still looking for that same item."

Nikki suddenly burst into tears. Sydney pulled her into her arms, holding her tight and reveling in the closeness. Since they'd been arguing for the past few months, she'd missed this contact with her sister. Who knew, maybe this would be a start to a better relationship between them.

Nikki pulled back. "You'll go with me to that place, right?"

The anguish in Nikki's eyes reminded Sydney of her sister's first day of kindergarten. In that situation, Sydney had had to let her sister grow up, but tonight she could afford to baby her a bit. "Of course I'll be there." She patted Nikki's shoulder. "Before we go we need to make a list of the things we want an officer to get from the house."

"How do I know what to bring if I don't know where we're going?"

"Pretend you're packing to spend the week at Emily's house."

Nikki's brow furrowed. "What about Emily's party tonight? Can I still go?"

Sydney couldn't believe she was asking. "Only if this guy is caught by then."

"This's so, like, not fair." Nikki crossed her arms. "You're the meanest person ever."

Sydney didn't have a comeback, so she sighed. "Make the list, okay?"

"Fine."

So much for their reconciliation.

As Nikki jotted down the essential items she'd need for the next few days, Sydney did the same, occasionally glancing at Russ. He stood near an unmarked sedan, his back to her, talking with two of his men. Unease still fluttered in her stomach, but his confident stance never wavered. It spoke to his internal strength and leadership skills with his men.

She knew her training and limited experience should give her some confidence in keeping herself and Nikki alive, but as the officers prepared to escort them out into the open, where the killer could lie in wait, doubt settled in.

She should be trusting God as she'd done on the way over here. After all, He was all-powerful. He could cocoon them in a blanket of safety, but fearful thoughts that even with Russ's help this man would track them down and kill them won out.

Eyes alert for trouble, Russ piloted his cruiser toward Valley View. After loading the bags brought back by one of his officers, putting a bulletproof vest on Nikki and settling the pair on the floor in the backseat, he'd departed the garage in a caravan of police vehicles.

Now, near the outskirts of town, starting with the car in the rear, one by one his men peeled off and sealed off roads. Not that any cars had challenged them.

"This is so lame. Can we sit up yet?" Nikki complained.

He heard Sydney groan her frustration. He stifled a similar response to Nikki's continued surly tone.

At thirty-three he didn't often feel old, but spending time with Nikki proved it had been a long time since his high-school days.

He wondered if Sydney remembered when she'd been Nikki's age and had confidently gazed up into his eyes, declaring she'd love him forever. He was sure her memories were far different from his.

What he remembered most was the way she'd furrowed her brow, the silver ring curling through her eyebrow wiggling, when he'd told her he wasn't interested. Well, and if he was being totally honest, how her legs had looked so incredibly long below denim shorts as she'd stomped away from him.

His cell phone rang, startling him.

"Stupid," he muttered under his breath for letting memories distract him from the job at hand.

He retrieved the phone and glanced at caller ID to see if he wanted to take the call now or wait until Valley View. When he spotted Garber's name, he clicked Talk. "What's up?"

"Thought you'd want to know. We've run down the cell phone. The registration was bogus, as expected."

"Any other news?" Russ asked.

"Yeah," Garber answered. "I had that talk with Eustis about Dixon's computer. He denies having it. Said someone must've planted it at his house to frame him."

Russ snorted. "He's been watching too many cop shows on TV."

Garber laughed. "Hopefully the computer will tell us something."

"We should have a chance to look at it tonight. Keep me posted on any new developments." Russ clicked off and relayed the news to Sydney, who offered no response.

Wondering what she was thinking, he made the turn onto the Pinetree Resort's driveway. His brother Ryan and Ryan's wife, Mia, owned the property that sat next to Valley View. Very few people were aware of the lake road leading from Pinetree to Valley View. If someone had managed to tail them, they'd think he was going to Pinetree.

Normally he'd worry about putting Mia and Ryan in danger, but they were expecting their first child in two months and had taken one last vacation before the baby was born. They weren't due home until tomorrow morning.

The car rumbled over deep ruts on Pinetree's unpaved driveway, bringing them to the lake road.

He called over his shoulder, "Okay. You can sit up now."

He heard the pair moving around, Nikki whining a few times. In the mirror, he saw Sydney's head pop up first, followed by her sister's.

"What're we doing at Pinetree?" Sydney asked.

He explained his reasoning.

"Good thinking," she said.

He hated to admit it, but her sincere compliment slid over him like a warm blanket. This crazy reaction to her had to stop for so many reasons. Why he couldn't keep a rein on it baffled him. Especially since he knew she'd run screaming in the other direction when she found out about his past.

He turned into Valley View's driveway and then swung the car as near to the grand lodge as possible and parked.

"Stay here until I come for you." He made sure his tone brooked no argument and climbed from the car.

He let his gaze sweep over the log lodge sitting in a cleared section of pine trees. Though he couldn't see through the closed plantation shutters on the large windows, he knew his always dependable brother waited for them.

Not taking time to let memories of his childhood home distract him, he took the steps to the wraparound porch two at a time, opened the door and called for Reid. He didn't take his eyes off the car, but heard footsteps coming down the large staircase from the second floor.

"We all set?" Russ asked.

"We're clear," his brother answered.

"I'll bring them in." Russ returned to the car and opened the door. "Head straight inside."

Both women, slightly bulkier from the vests they wore, got out without arguing and hurried to the door. The quiet, minus the stirring of the massive pines surrounding them, raised Russ's alarms. More disturbing was Sydney's easy cooperation.

Something was going on in that stubborn head. He dreaded what she might be planning.

By the time Russ returned to the porch, Reid had stationed himself on the far end of it. Good. This area was the most vulnerable for attack.

Reid's serious expression and alert eyes comforted Russ. It was good to have two people with the agenda of keeping these women safe. And, Russ hated to admit it, but two people who knew what it was like to kill someone in the line of duty. He was seriously beginning to think it might come to that before this situation ended.

He jerked his head at the door and Reid left his post to enter the lodge. Once inside with the door closed, Russ turned to his brother.

"You remember Sydney Tucker." He gestured in Sydney's direction.

Reid's sober expression softened. "Good to see you again, Sydney." He held out his hand and grinned in a way that Russ knew always melted women's hearts.

Sydney returned the smile and shook Reid's hand.

Russ sucked in a breath. He hadn't seen her face light up like that in years. The softness showed vulnerability that he hoped the killer wouldn't exploit.

"Are we gonna stand here all day." Nikki scowled.

Sydney's smile disappeared. Reid patted her shoulder as if telling her it was okay that Nikki had been rude. Since Nikki had helped Jessie last year, Reid thought Nikki could do no wrong.

"Good to see you again, kiddo." He wrapped an affectionate arm around her shoulder.

Nikki looked up at him. "Where's Jessie?"

"At home."

"Can she come over?"

Reid glanced at Russ then back at Nikki, his face apologetic. "Sorry. It's not a good idea for Jess to come over here right now."

Nikki glowered at Sydney. "I get it. I'd be a bad influence on her."

"What?" Reid asked.

She slipped out from under Reid's arm. "It's okay…I understand. I've been messing up."

"It's nothing like that, Nikki. Jess is only nine. Even if we tell her to keep this a secret, she might let it slip."

"Right." Nikki's sullen tone said she didn't believe him.

Russ stepped closer to her and connected gazes. "I've been straight with you, right?"

She nodded.

"Reid's telling you the truth. This doesn't have anything to do with you." He tipped his head. "Okay?"

She studied him. He held his breath as he waited for her agreement. For a reason he didn't want to identify, he wanted Sydney to see he'd connected with Nikki and that she trusted him.

"Okay," she whispered reluctantly.

"Good." He felt unbelievably happy over her agreement, but he had a job to do, so he stifled the feeling and nodded at the sofa sitting far away from a window. "You two have a seat. We'll get your bags."

"You don't need to carry my stuff. I can get it." Sydney jutted her jaw out, looking more like Nikki at this moment than she'd ever realized.

He didn't want to scare Nikki or he'd tell Sydney how dumb it was to put herself back in the killer's line of sight. "You've had a rough day. I'll get the bags."

"But I can—"

"I'll get them." Russ accompanied his statement with the stare he'd developed to get suspects to co-operate. She backed up and he hated the way her eyes reflected hurt.

He turned to Reid. "Let's go."

Russ could've gotten the bags himself, but he hoped for a chance to talk to Reid about Sydney's request for a separate safe house for Nikki.

Outside, he made sure the door latched behind Reid and followed his brother down the stairs.

Reid locked eyes with him. "You didn't tell me something was going on between you two."

"What're you talking about?"

"I thought you were a good cop, little brother. You'd have to be blind to miss the undertones in the sparring that just went on."

"Nothing's going on with us." He surged ahead and unlocked the trunk.

"Maybe not with actions, but your face gives you

away." Reid reached into the trunk for a tote bag. "Not a good thing when you're charged with her protection."

"Look." Russ peered over his shoulder at his brother. "She might be attractive, and, yes, maybe I could be interested, but nothing is happening between us."

"It wouldn't be a bad thing once this's over, though. It's time you started dating again."

"Seriously? We're not gonna have this conversation, are we?"

Reid laughed. "You're starting to turn into an old curmudgeon, so someone needs to tell you to get over what happened and move on with your life."

"I'm not doing this. Not now." Russ went to the front seat and grabbed Dixon's computer, leaving Reid to close the trunk and lug both of the bags.

"Someday you'll wake up and realize your job isn't enough anymore, bro," Reid called after him. "That you've wasted years when you could've been happy. With all that's going on with Sydney, I'd think you'd understand how precious life is."

Oh, he knew life was precious. So precious that he couldn't ever forgive himself for failing to protect Willie. He wouldn't let Reid sidetrack him from the job of keeping Sydney alive. She was a big enough distraction all on her own.

Sydney came down the stairs from making a security check and circled the room, checking the window locks. She was certain Reid had already made the rounds, but she needed something to do while the men were outside other than worry about her little sister.

A little sister who was already bored stiff. She wandered aimlessly though the room, picking up books and magazines and dropping them in disgust.

Sydney sighed and settled on the sofa. She was failing her sister…unlike Russ. He'd somehow found a way to connect with her.

Truth be told, Sydney was jealous. So jealous that instead of being grateful that he could communicate with Nikki, she'd snapped at him when all he wanted to do was get her bags. She knew she shouldn't go back outside, but she'd wanted to be in control of something.

Ha! As if she was in control of anything right now.

"Where's the TV?" Nikki asked.

Sydney looked around the room. "Doesn't look like there is one."

"You've gotta be kidding. I bet that means there's no internet either." Nikki sighed out a torrent of air. "This's so lame. What am I gonna do here?"

"You brought stuff to do, right?"

"Yeah, but I can't live without the internet." She dropped onto the sofa so hard the cushion next to Sydney popped up.

"You could read."

"Read what?" She stabbed a finger at the coffee table. "That Bible? As if."

Sydney let Nikki's comment drop. She wouldn't get into another argument with her sister, who'd also decided religion wasn't her thing. Nikki believed in God, but she didn't think she needed to go to church or youth group anymore.

The door whooshed opened.

Sydney clamped her hand on her gun and swiveled. She expected Russ and Reid, but the possibility existed that it could be the killer.

Heart thumping, she watched the brothers enter. Reid set their bags near the stairs. Russ, after double-checking the dead bolt, put Dixon's computer on a small table in the corner.

It wasn't hard to see they were brothers, especially if you looked at their matching blue eyes. Reid actually looked like and had the same build as Ryan, the youngest of the brothers. Russ was the tallest of the three incredibly attractive men and the only one who'd ever been able to melt her heart with one glance.

But she wouldn't let the way his warm gaze settled on her face right now, making her feel safe, allow her to let her guard down around him. Too much was at stake.

"This's so boring," Nikki lamented. "Can I go to my room?"

Russ headed her way. "Let me cover a few game rules first."

"Yay, rules." Nikki crossed her arms.

"They'll keep both of you safe if you follow them." Russ lifted his index finger. "First, no going outside. At all. Ever."

Nikki rolled her eyes and slumped deeper into the sofa.

"Second, stay away from windows. Keep them closed, blinds and curtains drawn at all times. Third, no phone calls, no texting, no internet."

"What?" Nikki shot up. "Why can't I talk to my friends?"

"Because you might accidentally tell them something that will give away our location."

"I'm not nine like Jessie. I know how to keep a secret."

"I need you to accept this, Nikki," Sydney said, hoping her authority would work.

"Fine. But I can't just ignore my friends. What am I gonna tell them?"

"Send one text. Tell them you've gone out of town with Sydney, and you'll talk to them when you get home." Russ nodded at the door. "And of course I probably don't need to tell you to keep the door locked. Don't open it to anyone but us."

"Can I go to my room now?" Nikki snapped.

"After I secure the upstairs."

"I already did that," Reid and Sydney chimed in together.

"I'll do it again." Russ frowned and headed for the stairs.

"This's stupid." Nikki got up and flounced across the room to a leather chair where she pulled out her iPod and plugged in her earbuds.

Russ grabbed the bags and climbed the stairs two at a time. The heavy bags didn't seem to weigh him down at all. Not that his physical strength should surprise her. She knew from when he'd rescued her last night that the man was rock-hard muscle. Not only was he a better law-enforcement officer, but she was inferior in strength, as well. Still, she would appreciate it if he would treat her more like a fellow officer.

She sighed out her frustration.

"You don't know much about him, do you?" Reid crossed the room and perched on the far end of the sofa.

She looked up at him. "Why do you say that?"

"If you did, his checking the upstairs wouldn't bother you so much."

"I'm not bothered."

Reid laughed. "Tell that to someone who isn't trained to observe body language."

"Fine. It irks me that he doesn't trust my judgment as a deputy." Her upset tone surprised her.

"It's not that he doesn't trust you." Reid's eyes sobered. "Believe me, I know. He trusts me, but he still had to check things out even after I cleared it."

"Then what's this all about?"

He looked up the stairs, at Russ standing on the landing, and smiled, his fondness for his brother evident. "That's something he needs to tell you about. I suggest you talk to him. Tell him how you feel."

She watched Russ start his descent, his brow tight with concentration. His gaze landed on her and a flash of protectiveness flared in his eyes. His expression said he would do anything to keep her safe. The same as she would do for Nikki.

Maybe Reid was right. Maybe this wasn't about him not trusting her. Maybe she should talk to Russ.

His expression turned suspicious. "What're you two up to?"

"Can I talk to you for a minute?" she asked.

He gave Reid a pointed stare. Reid returned it with a satisfied smile. The interchange between brothers was quick, so quick she wasn't sure she'd seen it, but the message was clear. Russ wanted Reid to stay out of his business. Reid had no intention of doing so.

Reid stood. "Hey, Nikki. Let's go to the den and I'll show you why I'm the Uno champ in our family."

Nikki jumped up. "Finally! Something to do." She stomped off and Reid followed.

Eyes narrowed, Russ took a seat in a chair across from her. "So what did Reid put you up to?"

"He didn't put me up to anything. He just suggested I talk to you." She tried to inject some nonchalance into her tone but could tell from his expression that she hadn't managed it very well.

"What's this about, Syd?"

He didn't miss anything. She'd best just come out with it. "I know I'm a rookie and I haven't demonstrated much competence in the job." She took a breath to go on.

"Not so. Your collar of Eustis today will be talked about around here for some time." He ended with a smile.

It felt like a ray of sunshine beaming at her, urging her to tell him how she felt. "It bothers me when you don't trust my judgment. Like just now. I cleared the upstairs and you couldn't let it go at that. You had to double-check."

The curve of his mouth flattened into a resolute slash. "That had nothing to do with you, Syd."

"Then what's going on?"

"Just a habit I picked up on the job."

"So tell me about it. Maybe it's a habit I need to embrace."

He rolled his eyes. "I need to remember you don't ever give up."

"Exactly. So save yourself some time." She put a teasing tone into her voice. "Tell me what's going on."

"Fine. When I was a rookie, my training officer searched a kid high on crack. He tossed him in the back of the car and we headed for lockup. But he missed a knife. The kid stabbed it through the screen. Sliced my shoulder. From that day on, even if my partner searched a suspect, I made it a habit to do another one."

"So that's why you double-check everything?"

She expected him to nod and be done with the conversation, but his eyes darkened and a myriad of emotions charged across his face until indecision won.

She'd never seen him indecisive about anything. Unease over what he hadn't said ground at her stomach. "Is there something about our killer that you're not telling me?"

"What? No…nothing like that." He got up, went to the kitchen counter and planted his hands on the countertop.

She followed. Laid a hand on his shoulder and he spun. Their eyes met and she saw the same gut-wrenching pain he'd shown at the hospital.

Something had wounded him deeply and it wasn't just the stab to his shoulder. It was something more serious and she wanted to help. "What is it, Russ?"

He removed her hand and held it between his, turning it over and studying it for long moments as if he was trying to come to a decision.

"Let's sit." He twined his fingers through hers and led her to the sofa.

When they sat, he loosened his grip as if to let go. She clung tighter to let him know that whatever he said, she'd support him.

He pulled in a deep breath. She squeezed his fingers to urge him to speak.

"The day of my son's fourth birthday, Wilson—my partner at the time—and I arrested a murder suspect. It was almost time for our shift to end and arresting this guy meant tons of paperwork to complete. The job had kept me from so many family events already. I didn't want to miss Zack's party. So I skipped that second search." He extricated his hand and lifted it to the back of his neck. "The suspect had another gun. Wilson missed it. When I hauled the suspect out of the cruiser, he opened fire. He hit a kid. Willie Babcock. He was only six. He died in my arms."

She could feel the anguish oozing from his pores. This tragedy had occurred a few years ago, but the pain in his voice said he still felt it as if it had happened yesterday.

"I'm so sorry, Russ. That must be hard to live with." She laid a hand on his knee. "Now I understand why you've been so sympathetic about my mistake with Dixon."

"I should have told you last night. Maybe it could've helped you even more."

"That's okay. You're telling me now."

He jumped up again. Paced the room. This had been hard for him to confide, but he'd shared a part of himself. That spoke volumes about his level of trusting her. She felt so close to him right now and wanted to show him how much this meant to her. Maybe how much he was starting to mean to her.

She went to him and met his gaze. "That wasn't so bad, was it?"

He let his eyes settle on her face and didn't say anything. He didn't have to. His expression said that he hadn't told her the whole story. He was holding something back, something that troubled him as much as the loss of this child. Something she wasn't brave enough to probe deeper to find. She wanted to reach up, touch his face, tell him she would understand no matter what.

But she didn't need to know anything else about him. Didn't need to get any closer. It would only lead to despair when he told her he didn't want to be tied down by a relationship that came with all of her responsibilities.

She walked away and went toward the table holding Dixon's computer. She was far better off focusing on work than on Russ. And better off remembering that he was off-limits. She knew that. Logically. But as she crossed the room, her heart ached and it was all she could do to keep moving.

TWELVE

Knowing Sydney could tell he hadn't told her everything, Russ watched her settle behind Dixon's computer. Even without telling her about his alcoholic past, he knew she'd seen something in his eyes that made her turn and walk away.

Good. Right?

It dissipated the warm sense of homecoming that had flooded his heart when she'd sat next to him on the sofa and encouraged him to confide in her, replacing it with a hard knot in his stomach.

Well, too bad if his gut ached. He needed to let these feelings go. Keep his focus on his job. He couldn't imagine how their killer would know her location, but her earlier assessment that their suspect was more inclined to abduct her than kill her, kept nagging at his gut. Enough so that he ordered Baker to stand guard outside for the night while he and Reid staffed the inside.

What was really bothering him was the suspicion that once the killer abducted Sydney, this creep would torture her to gain the information he sought. When she couldn't produce it, he'd end her life. But Russ wouldn't let him take her. He'd stand guard outside her door all night to watch over her.

He went to the kitchen and started a pot of strong coffee brewing so he would be alert all night. As he waited for it to brew, he looked over the rooms where he'd grown up. Nothing had changed since his parents retired to Florida. Reid had remodeled other parts of the resort, but he'd left the main lodge alone and rented it only to special groups.

Their parents stayed here when they visited. When the whole family gathered around the floor-to-ceiling stone fireplace in the family room, Russ could almost believe his life would someday return to normal. Then he left the security of his family, faced the very real problems of his past and wondered if he could ever have a normal life again.

Simple things, like the fun camaraderie between Reid and Nikki. As he waited for his coffee, the two returned from the family room complaining of hunger, pushed Russ out of the way and heated frozen meals before plopping down at the dining table to eat and resume their Uno game.

Russ leaned against the counter, sipping his coffee and enjoying the sound of Nikki's laughter as she soundly trounced Reid. Sydney looked up with a smile and crossed over to stand next to Nikki. Gazing down at her sister, her face filled with happiness.

Russ's not so much. His heart ached at the sight.

For a long time, he hadn't thought he needed something like this, but now he could see himself at home with Zack and a woman like Sydney beaming down on him. When he'd let the bottle take over his life, he'd blown his chances at a future like this. Now, when he could be hoping for something with Sydney, the bottle stood between them, too.

But wishing wouldn't change anything and there was no sense in dwelling on it.

He poured a fresh cup of coffee before crossing the room to talk to Reid. His brother studied his face with the assessing eyes of an FBI agent.

"I hate to break this up, but can I talk to you in the den, bro?" Russ asked in a lighthearted tone.

Reid slid the cards toward Sydney. "You might as well take my place." He ruffled Nikki's hair. "She's skunked me too many times."

"Oh, yeah," Nikki taunted. "And I'll do the same thing to you." She smiled a dare at Sydney.

Sydney slid into the chair. "We'll see about that, kiddo."

Wishing he could find some joy in this day, Russ led the way to the den and closed the door behind Reid, who settled into their Dad's favorite leather chair.

Russ set his coffee on a table to cool and went to the window to confirm that Baker remained outside before taking the chair opposite his brother.

"Stop worrying," Reid said. "We prepared for every contingency. We're as secure as can be."

"*As we can be* is the thing that's got me uneasy. Sydney's too unpredictable for me to rest easy," he groused, picking up his cup and watching the steam curl into the air.

"How'd your talk with her go?"

"Thanks for that, by the way."

Reid grinned in the way that Russ had hated as a kid. "Ooh, he evades the question. Don't tell me you didn't tell her about your past?"

"I did."

"But?"

"Just about Willie. Not how I handled it."

"No way you'll move forward with her until you tell her the whole story."

Russ knew Reid was right, but he wasn't planning to move forward with Sydney. She was the last person he wanted to saddle with his past. Someone like her deserved a whole man. One who hadn't treated his ex-wife badly and neglected his son.

And he didn't want Reid to try to convince him that he was deserving. He'd only feel hope then remember why he didn't deserve it. "Sydney asked me to find a separate safe house for Nikki and Kate."

"Nice change of subject."

"Can you find a place?"

A raised eyebrow was Reid's only comment on Russ's continued evasion. "Makes more sense to combine resources and keep them together."

"I agree, but if we don't comply with her wishes, she'll worry about them. I'm not sure she won't take off just to keep them safe." As thoughts of her strong will filled his mind, Russ smiled. "She clearly has a mind of her own."

"Just what you need, little brother, to get you back in the dating game. A woman who tests you all the way."

"We're talking about protection here, not dating."

"I know. I'm just saying I like what this woman is doing to you."

"Enough, all right? I'm serious—I don't want to talk about this." His sharp tone brooked no argument. "But I do want your help in locating a second safe house. Can you call in a favor and arrange a place or do I need to look on my own?"

Reid studied Russ for an uncomfortable length of time. Reminded him of when they were kids and Reid caught Russ in the act of doing something wrong. Well, Russ was older. Wiser. He wouldn't squirm.

He stared back. "Go ahead. Say what you're thinking."

"Is it such a good idea for you to continue to head up this case? Even if you won't admit it, it's clear you're getting too close to Sydney to make sound decisions."

Russ wanted to tell Reid that he could be objective and handle it, but was that true? Was his judgment impaired? Maybe she'd be better off under someone else's supervision.

Maybe...but the thought of sending her where he couldn't watch over her didn't sit well. For now, she'd remain in his care. The second he determined he was a liability to her, then and only then would he recuse himself from the case.

"Just make the arrangements." He left the room before Reid said anything else.

He went down the hallway to tell Sydney that Reid would work on locating another safe house. He found her on her knees, laughing hard as she slammed cards down in rapid-fire. Nikki's laughter joined her sister's and he couldn't help but smile along with them. This was the way the two of them should get along all of the time.

Unfortunately, he was here to tell them that he'd be splitting them up. Once Sydney told her sister about the pending separation, he predicted an end to this good time.

"Uno." Nikki tossed down a yellow card.

"Oh, yeah." Sydney dropped a wild card on the pile and announced a color change to red.

"And that, my dear sister, is how the game is won." Nikki slapped down a red three. Her lips curled up in an impish grin reminiscent of Sydney's younger days.

The memory of her face peering up at him with nothing but admiration and pent-up longing, left him wishing he could go back to the time when life was innocent. Before he messed things up.

Was Reid right? Had he totally crossed a line? Did he want her to look at him like she had when she was a starry-eyed schoolgirl? If so, he'd have to work hard to keep from showing his emotions as he'd never put her through that kind of crushing disappointment again.

Watching Russ from the corner of her eye, Sydney clicked through files on Dixon's computer. Since he'd returned from his discussion with Reid, he'd openly watched her as if he wanted to talk, but seemed afraid to approach her.

So she'd made herself available by joining him in the kitchen and initiating a conversation, but he responded to her comments with one-word answers and seemed almost uncomfortable in her presence. Then when Nikki invited him to play Uno, he jumped at the chance.

Sydney wasn't certain why she even wanted to talk to him, but his troubled expression made her want to help. So much, that it frightened her. But he'd made it clear that he didn't want her help, so she needed to let it go. Return to her work.

She focused on the computer screen. She'd love to have internet access to see what Dixon had been doing before his death, but that wasn't an option. An email icon sat on the desktop and she recognized it as a program where he'd download the emails for his provider's server, so she should be able to see his messages even without the internet. That is if he didn't have it password-protected.

She clicked on the icon and it opened his email account.

"Yes." She shot up her fist.

She scrolled down the listing. Found several emails addressed to Nikki's friends inviting them to parties. Sydney dreaded what she might find, but these emails seemed like the best way to track Dixon's moves. She read message after message. Learned nothing new except that Dixon thoroughly enjoyed corrupting young girls.

Farther down the list, she opened an email to Nate Johnson, Dixon's boss.

I have proof. You better believe I'll blow the whistle if you don't cooperate.

She clicked on an attached picture showing an invoice for plumbing materials.

"How's it going?" Russ asked.

Surprised to hear his voice so close, she looked up. He stood on the other side of the table and Nikki had gone to the kitchen to make popcorn.

Sydney pointed at the computer. "I'm in Dixon's email. It looks like he's blackmailing the construction foreman."

"Let me see." Russ came around the table and bent over her shoulder.

She clicked to the message and then the picture. "I don't know what this invoice proves, but it must mean something to Johnson. If Dixon was blackmailing Johnson, it's certainly motive to kill Dixon."

She leaned back and looked up at Russ. He didn't move away. She could see tiny flecks of gold in his eyes as he studied her. She should move back, but kept gazing into his eyes while imagining what it would be like to kiss him.

He suddenly drew in a deep breath and moved to the other side of the table. Sitting, he let out a long sigh. His phone pealed in a different ringtone than she'd heard on his other calls.

"My son." A smile, joyous and tender, lit his face as he lifted the phone. "Hi, Zack."

He talked with Zack about his day and what sounded like an upcoming weekend visit. She'd not heard him this cheerful since high school. She studied him as he talked. Love for his son was evident in every word. As was a deep longing in his eyes—to see Zack more often? She felt a burning desire to know what happened in his marriage to separate him from a child he clearly adored. She couldn't imagine his pain. She wasn't Nikki's biological parent, but if someone took Nikki from her, she'd grieve as Russ must be doing.

He ended the call, his expression warm and soft

as he peered at Sydney. "Sorry about that. I don't get to see Zack enough so when he calls, I drop whatever I'm doing."

"How old is he?"

"Seven going on twenty." His smile broadened.

"You really miss him."

"Yeah. A lot." His voice caught.

"What happened, Russ?"

A muscle twitched in his jaw. "What do you mean?"

"With your ex-wife and son?"

His smile disappeared. He hung his head forward and rubbed the back of his neck. "It was my fault. Every bit of it."

"You don't have to talk about it if you don't want to. I mean, it's none of my business."

He looked up and opened his mouth to speak, but then peered at her for a long silent moment as if he reconsidered speaking. She gave him an encouraging smile.

"I couldn't handle Willie Babcock's death," he said in a flat tone and peered at his hands. "It ate at me every day. So I started going out after work with some of the guys. Drank a little too much. That helped me forget. But then I'd get up in the morning and there it was again. That awful, nagging feeling that I'd cost this child his life. I started drinking in the day to wash away the pain."

She ached with compassion. "This child dying wasn't your—"

"Don't." His head shot up. "Don't say it wasn't my fault. I know that up here." He stabbed a finger at his temple. "But I can't reconcile it in my heart. So I drank to forget. In the process, I let down the two people I cared about most. Amy and Zack."

She understood. More than he could know. Dixon's death had given her an insight most people could never know. Yet she couldn't imagine the pain of seeing a child gunned down. And she couldn't imagine losing her family on top of it.

Before thinking stopped her, she got up and went around the table. She knelt in front of him and took his hands in hers. "I can't say anything to make you feel better. All I can say is I can't imagine how much pain you were in."

"I still am, Syd. I may have quit drinking, but the regret and pain over Willie's death still haunt me." He reversed their hands, turning hers over to study them. "Willie wasn't a drug dealer like Dixon. He was an innocent boy with his whole life ahead of him." His voice broke. "I think about Willie's parents every day. Wonder how they're doing and know that they hate me beyond belief."

"Have you ever talked to them about it?" she asked softly.

"No, I couldn't face them."

"You need to."

Sheer anguish filled his face, and he shook his head.

"When this is over, I'll go with you to see them if you'd like."

"Why would you do that?" He searched her eyes.

"Because after what happened with Dixon, I have a small idea of what you must be going through. You shouldn't spend the rest of your life tormented by something that wasn't your fault. This could be the way to let it go." She squeezed his hands.

"I wish it was that simple, but that's only the half of it. I also let my ex-wife and son down. I can never get that time back or undo the hurt I caused."

"You're a wonderful man, Russ. A fantastic boss. And from your phone call just now, I can see you're a terrific father. You had a problem, but that doesn't mean you should spend your whole life paying for it. You deserve to be happy."

His eyebrows arched. "I never expected this, Syd. Not from you."

"Expected what?"

"Understanding."

"I know what it's like to feel responsible for the loss of another person's life, so how could I not understand what you're going through?"

"You've been pretty outspoken about your mother's problem with alcohol. I thought you'd feel the same way about me."

Surprise hit her upside the head. She could see so clearly why Russ had turned to alcohol. He was simply trying to erase pain. She could even see that he deserved a second chance. But her mother? Not her mother.

So why was it different? Why couldn't she identify with her mother's struggle?

Was it the cruel things she'd said? The harsh look in her eyes when she'd threatened to give Nikki away? Or the fact that she hadn't cared enough to come after them when they took off for Aunt Lana's house?

That Sydney couldn't understand. Moving beyond the hurt would take forgiveness. Something she wasn't sure she had the ability to offer.

Russ had said something to change the supportive look on Sydney's face to one filled with the same gut-wrenching pain he'd felt all these years. Did bringing up her mother make her realize the full ramifications of his past? Did it help her imagine the kinds of things he'd done to his family? The way he'd hurt people he loved?

She gave his hand a squeeze then went into the kitchen. He was so confused. Despite the anguish in her eyes, did the final squeeze mean she supported him? He had to know.

He followed her.

She opened the door to the fridge. "You want anything?"

He shook his head and settled on one of the wrought-iron bar stools he and his brothers had occupied so frequently growing up. She pulled out a cola then filled a glass with ice.

He waited until she could hear him over the sound of clinking ice from the dispenser so Nikki wouldn't hear the conversation. "Can we talk about what just went on between us, Syd?"

"I'd rather not." She poured the soda over ice, droplets fizzing into the air. "Have you asked Reid to find another place for Nikki and Kate?"

He was disappointed in the subject change, but maybe she needed time to process his revelation. He'd honor her choice and move on. "He's making the arrangements, but it won't happen until tomorrow. It's best to hunker down here tonight and time the transfer to coincide with Kate's release."

Sydney's gaze drifted toward Nikki, who was playing solitaire. "I hate to ruin Nikki's good mood. Maybe I should wait until morning to tell her."

"I'm not sure that's such a good idea, Syd. We both know how she'll react. It would be best to let her blow off some steam tonight so tomorrow she's more compliant during the move."

"I guess you're right." She sighed. "I'll do it now, but be prepared for the fallout."

As Sydney went over to Nikki, her face tightened with sadness, making him wish he could change the turmoil the sisters were going through. While he was at it, change his past so he didn't have to wonder what Sydney was thinking about him. Their conversation showed him how much he'd come to care about her opinion of him. More than he wanted to admit.

"Let's go upstairs for a minute," she said to Nikki.

"But I'm having fun," Nikki whined.

Sydney peered down on her sister, a smile on her face, but Russ could still see the anguish in her eyes. "There's something I need to talk to you about."

"Fine, but I'm not going to bed this early." Nikki held up the deck of cards to Russ. "I'll be back to skunk you again."

Russ grinned at her. She might often have an attitude so big it was hard to see beyond, but he recognized it as the same determination Sydney had displayed in the old days. With Sydney's love and commitment to Nikki, she'd turn out to be a special woman, just like Sydney. A woman who deserved all the happiness in the world.

When they left the room, he went to Dixon's computer and peered at the plumbing supply invoice.

What about this invoice would allow Dixon to blackmail Johnson?

Russ scanned down the other email listings. Spotted additional emails to Johnson, all with a similar tone and attachments, except a few of them also had pictures of the actual construction of the town houses. Looked as if Johnson had violated building codes to save money. They needed an expert to look at these files.

Russ lifted his cell phone, called Garber and explained the situation. "I'm thinking Johnson was cutting corners and Dixon found out about it. I'll forward these emails to you. Contact the local building inspector. Bring him in ASAP to see if he can clarify the situation."

"Will do," Garber replied.

Russ disconnected and linked the computer to his phone by Bluetooth so he could send the files to Garber using his phone's connection to the internet. The process was time-consuming, but he wanted Garber to get on this right away.

As he sent the last message, Nikki stomped down the stairs and stormed past him without saying a word. As expected, she'd reacted poorly to the news. But his big question was how was Sydney handling it?

He imagined her sitting in her room, her face downcast over Nikki's reaction. Before thinking things through, he charged up the stairs and went to her room.

Empty.

Unease circled his brain. Russ lifted his weapon and eased down the hallway. Swung into each of the five bedrooms before finding Sydney asleep on Nikki's bed, Bible splayed open on her stomach.

He lowered his gun and hissed out his breath. He'd overreacted again. Sydney was the picture of innocence. He'd seen many sides of her, but not this one. Brash and outspoken in high school. Now tough and determined. Traits he could appreciate, but this sweetness emanating from her tugged hard at his heart.

He should just walk away, but finding her in the room he grew up in made him linger. She seemed as if she belonged in the space where he'd spent the first eighteen years of life. As if she was part of the family. The family that had stood by him in his time of need.

Would Sydney stand by him, or, after her history with her mom, would she run now that she knew the truth about him?

Run. Definitely run. As he should. In the other direction.

With a surprisingly heavy heart, he backed out of the room and silently closed the door. He'd rushed upstairs to be her knight in shining armor, but she didn't need a knight to rescue her from the same despair he often felt. She had her faith. Something he should consider exploring more. Especially after seeing how it was helping her through this terrible mess.

In the kitchen, he grabbed another cup of coffee and wondered how Nikki was handling the news. He couldn't resist the urge to check.

He found her in the den, curled up in an overstuffed chair with her cell phone clutched in her hand. She looked up and frowned. "If she sent you to talk to me, don't bother. The only one I want to talk to is Emily."

He couldn't have her calling a friend. No telling what she'd say in this mood. Maybe he should try talking with her. She'd opened up to him once. She could do so again. If she did, it might make things easier for Sydney.

"If by she you mean Sydney, I haven't talked to her." Russ sipped his coffee and waited for Nikki to start the conversation.

"This is so lame. I can't even call my friends." She slammed her phone onto the arm of the chair and slouched down.

"I'm guessing your friends can't take your call even if you could call them. They probably lost a few privileges after the officers arrived and arrested them for partying."

"Arresting them was so bogus. They weren't hurting anyone."

This wasn't the direction that would gain her understanding, but now that she'd raised the subject, he had a responsibility to see it through.

He sat on the corner of the large mahogany desk. "I won't lecture you on all the bad things drinking can do to your friends' bodies, but you need to think about what would happen if they climbed behind the wheel."

She shot him a look of superiority. "That's why I was there. Drinking makes me sick so I'm the designated driver."

"But you can't always be there for them. Sydney won't let you attend those parties."

"She might if she'd didn't think drinking was such a big deal," she retorted.

"But you don't think it's a big deal?"

"Well, yeah, sure. I mean, it's big enough to make our mom go all nutso. But not so big that we shouldn't give her another chance." She picked at a cuticle. "I wanna go see her, but Syd loses it every time I say anything about it. She won't even talk about it. So why bother trying?"

So this was the real reason behind Nikki's rebellion. He knew from experience if the mom hadn't sobered up, Sydney was making the right decision.

Nikki needed to know Sydney was doing the right thing. "She's trying to protect you from getting hurt again."

"As if. She's the only one who got hurt. She dragged me away from home when I was four. I don't remember anything."

"I'm sure Sydney's told you stories."

"Not really. Just said our life got all jammed up with Mom and we had to leave."

"And now you want to find out for yourself what your mother is like?"

"Well, yeah. I mean, so what if she has problems? She's my mother. I have a right to see her if I want to." Her eyes teared up.

"When you had your talk the other night, did you tell Sydney that?"

"I tried to, but when I brought up the party to tell her I wasn't drinking, she got all preachy. So I shut up." Nikki sighed. "She is, like, so hard to talk to."

"You still should've told her you weren't drinking, to ease her mind."

"Why should she get to feel good when she makes my life miserable all the time? She thinks she knows everything. Well, she doesn't. She had a mom and a dad… I never did." She sniffed. "It's too late for my dad, but a whacked mom is better than no mom at all."

Russ let Nikki's pronouncement settle over him. Children really did need their parents. Even at Nikki's age. Thankfully, after he'd recovered, his ex-wife had been understanding and had given him the chance to reestablish a relationship with Zack. Their bond grew stronger every time they were together.

If Sydney and Nikki's mom had recovered and was sorry for the way she treated them, she deserved the same chance. But with Sydney's feelings still raw from the situation, he doubted she would give her that opportunity.

THIRTEEN

Sydney flipped onto her side and sighed. She was too wide-awake to sleep. She'd tried to fall asleep for the past three hours, but the same impossible thought kept pummeling her brain. Plus that nap earlier in the evening hadn't helped either.

"Argh!" She ripped off the blankets and got up. On nights when she couldn't sleep, she found reading stilled her mind. So that's what she'd do. Make a cup of tea and read.

Fearing she might have to act suddenly, she'd remained dressed, minus her vest, so she simply slipped into her shoes and strapped on her duty belt. She wasn't going anywhere without her gun.

In the hallway, she found Russ seated in a plump chair blocking the top of the stairs. When they'd all turned in for the night, he'd told her either he or Reid would sit guard up here, so she wasn't surprised to find him, but after their emotional conversation she didn't know how she felt about seeing him.

The moonlight filtered through an upper window,

casting a long shadow over his face so she couldn't see if he was awake. Maybe he wasn't even aware she'd left her room. Hoping to tiptoe past him, she approached.

"Something wrong?" He shot to his feet.

She came forward. "Couldn't sleep."

In the light now beaming directly on his face, she could see the five-o'clock shadow that had darkened his jaw, giving him a dangerous, bad-boy kind of appearance. His sleepy yet interested gaze roamed her from head to toe and kicked up her heart rate.

From all her recent thoughts about him, she was probably imagining this interest. "I'm gonna make some tea. You want some?"

"Sure."

Now, why had she asked him to join her? That was just plain asking for trouble. She ran down to the kitchen, hearing his soft footfalls behind her, allowing her time to control her emotions.

How could a man who was wrong for her in every way still make her heart beat faster? So she was physically attracted to him. So what? Didn't mean she'd act on it. Unfortunately, her feelings went deeper than that. She was drawn to his kindness, his strength, his sensitivity to her needs. And that was so much harder to ignore.

She filled mugs with water from the tap and started the microwave. Picking up a basket with assorted teas, she turned and spotted Russ sliding onto a stool at the island.

She set the basket in front of him. "What kind do you want?"

He shrugged. "Doesn't matter. I rarely drink tea so you pick for me."

"Do you want me to make something else?"

"This is fine." He let his eyes linger on her face, almost like a caress.

She hadn't been wrong; he did seem to feel the same attraction. Despite knowing they could never be together, she liked the admiration she saw in his eyes. Liked it a lot. But she wouldn't spend any more time reveling in it.

She averted her eyes and dug though the basket until she found packets of chamomile. Chamomile relaxed and promoted sleep, but with the emotions flowing between them, no amount of tea would make either one of them sleepy.

The microwave beeped. She retrieved the mugs and settled one bag into a cup before sliding it across the island. She fixed hers and prepared to head to the den and away from those smoldering eyes.

He cupped his mug. "Since you can't sleep, maybe you'd like to hear about the conversation I had with Nikki earlier tonight."

So much for retreating to the den. "Once upon a time when I had a great relationship with her, I'd have jumped at the chance to hear what she had to say."

"But now?"

"Now I don't know." Sydney sighed. "Some days I

wish I could just be her sister. Not have to deal with the responsibility of raising her."

"I can't imagine how you do it. I mean, teenage girls bring so much drama. I couldn't handle something like that all the time."

She felt as if he'd jerked the rug out from under her. Just what she needed—a reminder that he didn't want to have anything to do with a woman who had the responsibility of a teenage girl.

But she needed to know what was going on in Nikki's head. "So go ahead. Tell me what she said."

"Okay, but promise me you'll hear the whole story before going off on me?"

This didn't sound good, but she couldn't avoid the truth. "I'll do my best."

"Well, the good news is that she doesn't like to drink. Said it makes her barf."

This *was* good news. "So why keep going to parties, then?"

"She's the designated driver. Says she can't stop her friends from partying and she wants to keep them safe."

"Seriously? I've been on her case about drinking for nothing?"

"Looks like it."

Sydney ran a hand through her hair, combing strands that had tangled while she'd tossed in bed. Maybe this would be the start of untangling her problems with Nikki, as well. "She must really be mad at me."

"Pretty much."

"So why didn't she tell me that?" she demanded.

"She said you overreact whenever alcohol is mentioned."

Sydney didn't even have to think about whether she was guilty of overreacting. When it came to her mother, she was the queen of overreaction. "I just don't want Nikki to turn out like our mother."

"Looks like that won't happen, doesn't it?"

"Yeah. At least for now." She couldn't help but feel relief and offered a quick prayer of thanks. "You said this was the good news. What's the bad?"

"I don't know if it's so much bad news as something you won't want to hear." He paused.

Anxiety mounted. "Tell me already."

"Nikki wants to have a relationship with your mother."

"We've already talked about this. I told her it wasn't an option. It never will be while I'm responsible for her." Sydney packed her words with vehemence.

Russ pulled back as if she'd slapped him. "Don't you want to think about this before taking such a rigid stance?"

"Absolutely not. No good will come of letting that woman into our lives."

"If you don't want to lose Nikki, you need to lighten up and listen to how important this is to her."

"How can I? Our mother wanted to give Nikki away. I can't tell her that."

"That was likely the alcohol talking," he reminded her.

The days and nights of her mother's drunken behavior played like a video in Sydney's mind. "You weren't there, Russ." As the pain resurfaced, her voice quieted. "You didn't see her eyes. Hear the conviction in her voice."

"But I have been there, Syd." His eyes saddened. "When you're under the influence of alcohol, you do and say things you'd never do sober."

"So I should excuse her, then?"

"Excuse? No. Forgive, maybe. Nikki deserves to find out for herself how she feels about your mother. If you don't let her see her mother, she may come to resent you. Then where will you be?"

Sydney heard the logic in his words and believed he could be right, but still couldn't fathom letting Nikki see the woman who'd wanted nothing to do with them.

"I'm sorry, Russ, but I can't talk about this right now. Especially not with someone who has the same perspective as my mother."

Sydney grabbed her mug and headed toward the den. She couldn't let their mother anywhere near Nikki. She'd only be a bad influence.

Her feet shuffled on the wood floor and echoed down the long hall, giving sound to her frustration.

Russ was sure to think she was mad at him, but she wasn't. She was upset over the situation.

Well, maybe she *was* mad at him. Mad about finding out the man she'd come to care for was in the same league as the mother who had wanted to throw her out like trash.

She glanced back at him. His face was tight with disappointment. Good. If he kept looking at her like that, she could easily avoid the pull that seemed to be drawing her to him.

Russ wished Sydney had been willing to continue her conversation with him, but she'd made it clear that his past kept her from trusting him. Maybe she was right. Maybe his intense desire for her to accept him skewed his perception. He was tempted to head after her and tell her how he felt, but a scraping noise from the porch grabbed his attention.

All senses suddenly alert, he focused on the floor-to-ceiling windows covered with massive plantation shutters. A moving shadow seeped through the slats. Someone was on the porch, stealthily heading in Sydney's direction.

He whipped his gun from the holster and called Baker on his mic.

Baker didn't respond.

Russ tried again. No response.

Something was wrong.

Gun arm outstretched, he raced toward the den. The room contained a door to the porch, giving the killer easy access. Russ wanted to shout at Sydney to take cover, but if the intruder didn't know her location, he'd draw attention to her. Better to keep quiet and move faster than the intruder.

Russ shoved open the door and quickly scanned the room. Sydney sat facing away from him, her back to the exterior door.

He flipped off the overhead light.

"Hey." She shifted to face him.

"Get down," he said in a low, warning tone as he charged toward her.

"What?" She remained in place, questioning him with her eyes.

"On the floor, now!" He turned off the reading lamp.

She dived for cover. He landed behind her, wrapped an arm around her waist and rolled until his body was between her and the door. "There's someone on the porch."

"Nikki." She rose up as if to leave.

He clamped his free arm tighter. "Reid's with her. We need to concentrate on getting out of this room safely, then we can check on her."

He felt her body relax. She wasn't wearing her vest. She'd counted on him to protect her and let her guard down. If he were a swearing man, he'd issue a curse so loud they'd hear him in town. But that wouldn't do either of them any good. He had to keep his head. Assess the threat.

He let her go and flipped to check the exterior

door flanked by two windows with the same shutters as in the family room. He didn't see any movement. Maybe he'd overreacted. Wouldn't be the first time an animal came onto the porch in search of food. But an animal wouldn't have taken out Baker.

Though the room was dark, he knew every inch of it. He could still smell the tobacco from the pipe his father smoked after dinner and visualize the walls lined with bookcases filled to brimming with books. They had a straight shot to the door, but there was nothing to protect them from a bullet on the way.

He felt Sydney moving behind him. Could tell she was turning to face the same direction.

"I don't see anything," she whispered, her breath warming his neck.

"We'll wait a few minutes to be sure."

"What exactly did you see?" she asked.

"A shadow moving past the family-room window headed this way."

"He could've already passed us on the way to the back of the house. There's another set of stairs back there. He could be heading for Nikki." Sydney rose up.

"Wait. We'll go together." Crouching, he led her by the hand into the hallway, where he stopped and listened. "He's still on the porch. Nikki should be fine."

"There could be two of them. We need to make sure Nikki's okay." He heard the desperation in her voice.

"With this guy still on the porch, it's too dangerous

to go through the family room. I'll call Reid." He eased out his cell. "We may have a breach. Check on Nikki."

"On it," Reid replied in a groggy voice.

"There's no one better than Reid to protect her." He set his phone to vibrate in case Reid called back—didn't want to alert the intruder with it ringing—and dialed his office to request assistance.

As he was talking, a window in the den shattered. He heard something thud to the floor. Not a body, something smaller.

"I need you here now!" he whispered into the phone. "Let's move," he said to Sydney.

Using his body as a shield, he pushed her down the hallway. Near the end of the hall, she bolted toward the family room, obviously heading for the stairs to check on Nikki.

He grabbed her arm. "Reid will handle things upstairs. I need you to do as I say now."

"But Nikki…"

"No buts, Syd. We'll wait down here." He directed her to a small bathroom under the stairs. He didn't like the situation one bit. They were sitting ducks, but this was the best option. He'd like to take a defensive stance in the hallway, but he was certain Sydney wouldn't stay inside alone.

"Now what?" she asked.

"We update Reid, then keep quiet so it takes longer to locate us. Then we wait for backup." Hoping to hear the wail of sirens soon, Russ made a quick call to Reid. Russ wished his brother could back them up, but he had his hands full monitoring two staircases leading to Nikki.

Time ticked by in slow increments. The only sound Russ heard was blood pounding through his head and Sydney's occasional deep breathing followed by a hissing exhalation. He could understand her feelings. If Zack were upstairs, nothing, not even another officer guarding the door, would make him settle down and wait this out. But thankfully, Zack wasn't upstairs.

A good thing, too. Russ needed to stop thinking about his son and keep his mind on protecting Sydney. With this latest intrusion, he needed to up his game to keep Sydney alive.

FOURTEEN

Sydney held her gun at the ready and tried to calm her breathing, but the more she thought about the in-and-out process, the harder it was to do. The room seemed to close in on her and she felt light-headed. What kind of deputy was she if this made her go faint?

C'mon, Sydney. Get a grip.

She took a deep, cleansing breath, but the wooziness persisted. She'd already prayed, but obviously she wasn't trusting God to care for them.

Father, please let me trust in Your protection.

As if God thought she needed a sign to help her through this, the wail of sirens curled through the air. They'd never sounded so good to Sydney. She hated to admit it, but even though she wanted to trust God, she'd been certain the intruder would kill Russ or Nikki to get to her. She didn't want to die, but she'd give up her life for them.

She stayed in her spot, listening as Russ phoned

his station and had the call routed to the approaching officer. He quickly updated him on the situation.

"We'll stay put until you give us the all-clear." He clicked off then phoned Reid and gave him the same information.

Sydney relaxed a bit, but they weren't out of the woods yet. The intruder could still be in the house, hoping to take one of them hostage as a means of escape. Russ's call could've alerted him to their location, but hopefully he'd taken off after hearing the sirens.

Additional sirens joined the lone wail. Good. She sighed in relief and felt her pulse start to calm. This was what they needed. A show of force.

She listened to cars squeal to a stop, footfalls pound up the steps and tread through the house with sounds of "clear" being called out. When fingers of light crept under the door and brightened their cave, Russ turned to her.

"You okay?" he asked with tenderness in his voice that melted her heart.

"I will be." Her voice shook as a shiver took hold of her body. All the fear she'd been suppressing reverberated through her tone.

He sucked in a breath and holstered his gun before crossing over and pulling her to him. Still holding her weapon, she relaxed against his broad chest and wrapped her free arm around his waist. As she inhaled his clean scent, residual fear hovering near the surface evaporated.

His arms loosened. She leaned back to look up at him. The warmth in his eyes stole her breath. He really seemed to care about her.

He smiled with the sweet little smirk that she couldn't resist. "If I'm gonna keep you safe, you need to not question my every move."

She'd expected anger and a harsh tone, but the only thing he telegraphed was the sincere desire to protect her, taking away all of her usual defenses.

"I want to trust you, Russ—" she let her gaze linger on his eyes "—but when it comes to Nikki, I—" Strong, almost primal, emotions took away the rest of her sentence.

He lifted a hand and ran his fingers tenderly along her cheek. "I understand, Syd. Just promise me you'll try."

"I will."

Their eyes locked. His adoring gaze overpowered the sensible impulse to push him away. His head dipped closer. He was going to kiss her. A wave of happiness eased out all fear. Warm and tender, his lips claimed hers. She clutched the back of his shirt. Lost her breath again. She released the fabric and reached up to his neck to draw him closer.

With a groan, he lifted his head. She sighed at the loss of contact and let her gaze connect with his again. She wanted him to kiss her again and could see the same longing on his face.

"All clear, Chief." A deep voice from the other side of the door placed a spotlight on all that was wrong with kissing Russ and felt as if a bucket of cold water had been tossed over her head.

Eyes still engaged with unspoken emotions traveling between them, her hand dropped. She took a few steps back. Russ pulled in a deep breath, paused for a moment, then turned to unlock the door. The light flooded in, ending a special moment that never should've happened.

"You find Baker?" Russ's voice was husky but all business now.

"Yeah," Garber answered. "The suspect knocked him out. He'll be fine."

Relief flooded Russ's face. "Bring me up to speed on what went down out here."

"A bomb was tossed through the den window," Garber said.

"Then we need to evacuate."

"It okay. Krueger checked it out. Said it was made of putty, not C4."

Russ knew all about Krueger's munitions expertise from his army days—the man told everyone who would listen how he'd defused every type of bomb. Still, Russ didn't want to take a chance. "Have him remove it from the premises."

Garber nodded then took off down the hallway.

Sydney's cell chimed. Certain it was from the killer, she didn't want to look at the text.

"You want me to look at it first?" Russ asked.

She shook her head and thumbed to the message. Russ leaned over her shoulder.

You can't hide from me, Deputy Tucker. I'm running out of patience. I suggest you give me what I want or the next time the bomb will be real.

"This's escalating out of control," she said. "How did he even know we were here?"

"We'll talk about this later." Russ nodded at her sister jogging down the stairs. "Nikki needs you right now."

Eyes wide like a frightened doe's, Nikki ran for Sydney and flung herself into Sydney's arms. She clutched the crying teenager and rested her chin on Nikki's soft hair. Reid followed down the stairs at a slower pace, his eyes tight with worry.

"A minute," he said to Russ and jerked his head for Russ to follow.

They walked away, leaving Sydney feeling alone and helpless.

Nikki looked up at Sydney. "You won't send me away by myself now, will you?"

"We'll see." Sydney stroked her sister's back as she did when she'd had nightmares as a child.

She trembled and Sydney's resolve to send Nikki to her own safe house wavered. She dug deep and found the strength that had allowed her to flee their mother. On that day, Sydney promised herself that she'd never let her sister experience such pain again.

Sydney had failed on that promise tonight. She

couldn't do it again or the consequences could be deadly. This maniac wanted something from Sydney, and Nikki didn't have to get hurt in the process. Nikki would go to the safe house alone as planned, but not tomorrow. Sydney would insist she go tonight.

Intent on telling Reid to move up the arrangements, she looked at him.

The brothers' heads were pressed together, their posture rigid. She was sure they were already discussing changes that this latest intrusion warranted. Now that the killer had breached the safe house, they probably wanted to take Sydney with them, too.

Russ caught her gaze, telegraphing the seriousness of the situation. She didn't need him to convey their dire straits. She'd put too many lives in danger. These two fine men had risked their lives to keep her and Nikki safe. She owed them both so much. And she owed it to them and Nikki to end this thing right now.

The chaos grew exponentially as Reid's associates arrived and swarmed like ants through the rooms. Sydney kept her cool, but the activity grew too taxing for Nikki, so Sydney sent her sister upstairs to pack. With Nikki out of the room, now was the time to tell Russ that even if he wanted her to go away with Nikki, she wouldn't be leaving.

She approached him as he talked with Reid. "I'm

sure the two of you are planning to send me off with Nikki, but I'm staying here."

"No way," Russ said.

"This episode proves Nikki needs to be as far from me as possible."

Russ's jaw clenched.

She knew he wouldn't budge no matter what she said, so she focused on Reid. "If you and Jessie were in this situation, what would you do?"

"If I was thinking rationally, which history has proven I don't do when it involves her, I'd like to think I'd send her away." Reid offered Russ an apologetic glance.

"And you'd stay here like a sitting duck?" Russ's voice rose.

"No, I wouldn't sit around. I'd bait the guy into showing himself."

Russ shot Reid an irritated glare. "Don't even think of doing that, Syd."

"Me?" she said, hoping her tone didn't betray the plan forming in her mind.

"See what you've done, man?" Russ said to Reid.

Reid chuckled. "Her guilty expression says she might already be planning to do so."

She pressed on before Russ chimed in with some crazy demand. "So we're agreed, then? Nikki will leave tonight, and I'll stay here."

"No, we're not agreed." Russ huffed out a breath of frustration.

She wouldn't let it stop her. "I don't think there's any way you can make me go."

He pierced her with a sharp stare. "You're right— I can't make you go. But I won't let you stay at the lodge. We'll find another place."

"And then what? Put someone else in danger, too? No, thanks." Her tone was as pointed as his stare.

Reid stepped between them. "You're both too close to the situation." He clamped a hand on Russ's shoulder. "Last year when Jessie was kidnapped, you kept me from doing something dumb. I'll do the same thing for you. As of this moment, I'm in charge."

"But—" Russ and Sydney both responded.

"No buts." Reid's tone was firm. "Give me a few minutes to confer with my associates, and I'll get back to you with a plan."

Sydney watched him walk away. She didn't know what he'd come up with, but no matter his plan, she'd move forward with hers. Even if Russ continued to gaze at her as if he'd like to lock her up and throw away the key.

"We need to talk." He directed her to the side of the room and out of the chaos. "You can't just go off on your own and bait this guy. He's proven how capable he is. Once he knows you don't have what he's looking for, he'll kill you."

"Maybe. Maybe not. But at least he won't hurt anyone else I care about."

"Nikki and Kate will be safe in Portland so he can't hurt them," he reminded her.

"What about you? How are you going to stop him from hurting you?"

"Are you saying you care about me?" he murmured.

Suddenly feeling shy, she looked at her feet. "I would think after that kiss, it would be obvious."

"I feel the same way, Syd." He slipped a finger under her chin and lifted her head. "That's why I can't let you do this. You may think baiting the killer will keep him away from me, but it won't. I'll do everything within my power to protect you. And trailing after you when you go off on your own would leave me more exposed than if we were hunkered down in a safe house."

"I don't know, Russ…"

"I've been in law enforcement longer than you. Trust me to do the right thing."

Everyone she'd ever cared about had let her down. She'd had to take over. To take care of herself and Nikki. Could she really trust Russ's decision?

He moved closer. "Syd?"

She could see the pain her indecision lodged in his eyes, but she couldn't blindly let someone take over caring for her and Nikki. Yet she didn't want to hurt Russ.

What should she do?

Seeking answers, she looked around the room.

Caught Reid's attention. He finished his conversation and crossed the room.

"We're all set. Nikki will go to Portland as planned. Russ and I'll transport you to another safe house."

"I won't put anyone else in danger, Reid."

"No need to worry about it. We're going to Claudia Umber's house. She's the former assistant special agent in charge of the Portland office. She retired a few years ago and moved out here. No one, and I mean no one, can get the best of her."

"Sounds like a plan." Russ trained his gaze on Sydney.

"Fine," Sydney said. She'd go along with them. If she found the arrangements would endanger anyone, then she could still take off as planned.

"Now, if you'll bring Nikki up to speed on the plans—" Reid paused and nodded at Nikki, who'd come downstairs and sat on the sofa with her backpack under her knees "—we'll get this transfer under way."

"Want help telling her you won't be going with her?" Russ asked. "She seems to trust me. I'll do my best to make sure this doesn't traumatize her."

She peered into his eyes. Eyes that were beginning to make her do things that she normally wouldn't consider.

"I don't know," she said.

"I promise not to say a word unless you ask me

to." His sincere desire to help was written all over his face.

Who was she to say no if it could help Nikki? "Okay, thank you."

Sydney went to the sofa and wrapped an arm around her sister's shoulder. "Ready to go?"

Nikki nodded. "Where's your stuff?"

"As much as I want to, I won't be able to go with you." Sydney squeezed Nikki's shoulder.

"What? Why not?"

Sydney explained their logic.

"I don't care," Nikki cried. "I want you to come with me."

"It'll be better for you if I don't."

"No, it won't!" Nikki jumped to her feet.

Hoping Nikki would process the info and come to realize it was the best decision, Sydney let her sister fume and sort out her thoughts.

She suddenly spun on Sydney. "Don't worry. I get it. You'd rather stay here and play cops. It's always about your job. Or the neighbors. Or you. Anybody but me." She crossed her arms. "It's never about me."

Sydney could barely stand the look of misery on her sister's face. She wanted to comfort her, but then she was afraid she'd give in and agree to go with her to the safe house.

To keep from reaching out to Nikki, Sydney

clasped her hands together in her lap. "This *is* about you, Nikki. I'm doing what I think is best for you."

"Right," Nikki said. "Abandoning me is best for me."

At a loss of what to say next, Sydney looked to Russ for help.

He faced Nikki. "Sometimes it's best for us to stay away from the people we care about."

Sydney could hear pain in Russ's tone but Nikki shrugged. "I expected you to be on *her* side."

"I'm not on anyone's side. I'm telling you the truth." He lifted her chin with his finger as he'd done to Sydney a few moments ago. She could still feel the imprint of his finger. Still wished she'd been able to look into his eyes and trust him, as Nikki seemed to be moving toward doing.

"I have a son," Russ went on. "He's seven, but I haven't lived with him for a few years."

Nikki's jaw dropped open. "Seriously? That's so lame."

Russ cringed. "You're right. It is lame. But at the time I left him, I was in no position to be a good father."

"Seems like you'd be a good dad to me."

Russ smiled as if he liked her vote of confidence. "I think I am. Today. But back then, I got into drinking. Messed everything up."

"Like my mom."

"Yeah, like your mom."

"But she didn't ditch us."

Sydney could see Nikki's comment worsened the pain already eating at Russ. But he kept the resolved look on his face. "I didn't ditch Zack, either. I was drunk and feeling sorry for myself all the time. How could I stay around him when I didn't want him to learn to do the same thing? I loved him too much for that. So I left." He sighed. "Your sister is doing the same thing. She cares too much about you to let you stay in this dangerous situation."

Nikki seemed to ponder his words. "You were really a drunk, huh?"

Sydney almost laughed with relief that Nikki was now more interested in the fact that Russ was an alcoholic instead of the safe-house assignments.

"One of the worst." Russ let his eyes settle on Sydney's face. "So bad my wife divorced me. Now I only get to see my son every other week."

At one time, she'd thought an admission of how someone had let alcohol ruin their life would send disgust churning in her stomach, but the way he'd faced his problem and recovered from it actually made her respect him more.

Nikki shook her head. "Just can't see you drinking. You're so uptight and Mister Lawman now." Her tone had lightened and was almost taunting.

His face didn't break in laughter. "I'd like to think I was too tough to let alcohol take over, but it can happen to anyone whose foundation is shaken badly enough and doesn't know how to deal with the problem the right way."

Sadness, maybe regret, on his face left Sydney with questions. Willie's death had affected Russ so much that he'd drowned his pain in a bottle. The same thing had happened to her mother—her father leaving had cut her mother to the quick and she'd sunk into despair.

Had Sydney been fair to their mother? If she'd fallen into depression instead of a drunken state, would Sydney have been more sympathetic? Should she reconsider her stance on their mother if she'd quit drinking as Russ had?

Reid rejoined them. "So are we ready to go?"

Thoughts of anything other than the madman chasing her vanished. As cunning as their foe was turning out to be, she had to keep her head in the game or the consequences could be dire.

FIFTEEN

Sydney peered out the living-room window of Claudia's rustic log home. The one-story building sat, secluded, in a dense forest of tall trees at the end of a long gravel driveway. Heavy fog clung to the ground, refusing to clear and let the sun break through.

Sydney kept vigil at the window, watching as dawn came and went along with the morning, ticking past in slow increments as she went stir-crazy. Not that Claudia hadn't been a gracious host. Quite the contrary: Sydney wished she'd met her under different circumstances and could talk with the older woman about her experience in law enforcement. And she wished she hadn't put her or the men in the line of fire.

Sydney peeked out the window to check on the men.

Reid stood at the end of the driveway, Russ on the porch. The main drive was the only entrance onto the property, so Sydney felt confident that even if the killer figured out their new location, he wouldn't get past Reid. Problem was what he might do to Reid.

"You shouldn't be by the window," Claudia said, coming up behind her. Tall, nearly six feet, and thin with silvery hair styled in a buzz cut, the woman commanded respect simply by the way she carried herself.

"For some reason, I feel claustrophobic here." Sydney let the drapes fall over the picture window.

"Probably because you want to be out there hunting down the killer before he hurts someone you care about."

"Did Russ tell you that?"

"Didn't have to. I've seen it in your eyes all day."

Could she also see Sydney's feelings for Russ, or was she hiding it well enough?

"Piece of advice?" Claudia offered.

"Sure."

"Stop worrying. It won't change anything."

"Easy to say, so hard to do." Sydney had tried to put her trust in God, but even with everyone safe for now, she'd failed.

"I hear you, but listen to an old broad like me. The older you get, the more you realize what a waste of time it is. Whatever's gonna happen, happens." She went to the hook by the door and retrieved a sheepskin jacket. "I'm going out to spell Russ and then Reid so they can grab something to eat and shake off the cold." She shrugged on the jacket over a berry turtleneck. "I know you want this to end and you think you're putting us all in danger, but don't do anything foolish while I'm gone."

When the door closed behind her, Sydney went to a leather club chair in front of the tall fireplace. She purposefully positioned her back to the door. A real no-no in the police world—always face the door so you can see any threat coming your way—but the threat she feared right now would wound her heart, not kill her.

She heard the door open and the sound of Russ's booted feet thumping across the wood floor to the kitchen. After the kiss and her admission of caring about him, she didn't know what to say if he came over. Whenever he looked at her with eyes all tender and warm, she wanted nothing more than to pursue a relationship with him. Not that she'd give in to her feelings. She still had Nikki to think about.

Sydney sighed out her anxiety. At least her sister was safe for now. She'd arrived in Portland and gone straight to bed. And Kate was safe, too. She'd called to say she was still in the hospital. During the night she started seeing double, so they were keeping her to determine if this was due to the head injury or an MS flare-up.

"Everything okay in here?" Russ asked from behind, startling her.

She pivoted. He held a steaming cup of coffee in

his hand. He fixed his eyes on hers and she felt the resolve to stay away from him instantly slip.

"Everything's fine." She looked at the fire snapping in the hearth.

"Really? Claudia said you're feeling a little claustrophobic."

"It'll pass."

He narrowed his eyes. "You're not planning anything foolish, are you?"

"No. I'll sit tight for now."

His cell rang and he set his cup on the table before lifting the phone. "What is it, Garber?" He listened intently. "When? Where?" A spark of energy flared in his eyes as he cupped his hand over the mouthpiece. "We may have the murder weapon."

Excitement propelled Sydney to her feet. She listened to Russ discuss ballistics with Garber. He smiled at her, and she caught his enthusiasm. This could be the big break they needed.

"Are you sure?" Russ asked, his expression turning sour. "Fine. Get the weapon to ballistics. I'll be there as soon as I work the logistics out here." He shoved his phone into the belt holder with excessive force. "They found a gun down by the lake. Looks like the murder weapon." He ended with a scowl.

"That's good news." She smiled. "So why are you so mad?"

"Why?" his voice shot up an octave. "I'll tell

you why. The gun is registered to you. Your service weapon, to be exact."

"What?" She felt the blood rush from her face and her knees go weak. She laid a hand on the fireplace mantel to steady herself and process the news.

"Care to fill me in on how it ended up by the lake?" Russ continued to glare at her.

She didn't like the look one bit. True, she'd side-stepped his questions about her gun, but that had been under her boss's direction. She'd never imagined someone would use it to commit murder.

"I didn't take it there, if that's what you're asking."

"So how did it get down by the lake?" His voice was low, his eyes watchful.

"I don't know, Russ."

"I asked you twice if you'd lost your duty weapon. You blew me off. Now I find out it could be our murder weapon." He assessed her coldly. "You better start talking and fast."

The officer in her sent out a defiant stare, hoping it came out much like Nikki's often did, but the woman in her grieved over how the man she cared about could so easily believe the worst about her.

She let the officer win and pulled back her shoulders. "As I told you at the murder scene, I took off my duty belt and put it in my backpack."

He held up a hand. "Let's cut to the part that you didn't tell me."

"Fine. When I got home, Nikki put the backpack

on my bed. After she took off, I went to get the gun. Discovered it was missing. I thought she'd taken it to get back at me."

"That explains why you patted her down," he clarified.

"Not my finest moment, but I couldn't let her get caught carrying. Turns out someone must have broken into my car while I was at the lake."

"And you didn't think this was important to tell me when I asked about it?" Disbelief laced his words.

"I had a responsibility to tell Sarge first, so I couldn't tell you then."

He leveled his gaze at her. "And did you report it to Krueger?"

"That's why I had to stop at the office first thing the other day."

"So when I asked you about it again, why didn't you tell me then?"

"Sarge ordered me to keep it quiet," she admitted. "He didn't want my careless actions to damage our department's good name."

He shook his head and marched toward the door where he paused. "You better hope the ballistics don't come back as a match. Even I can't stop the fallout that will cause."

She leaned against the mantel and watched him leave. She'd disappointed him again. More than disappointed. His final look told her he might never trust her again. Maybe never want to see her again, either.

A knife of pain, much like the one she'd felt when her father had left, sliced into her stomach. This pain only came from hurting someone you cared about. Flashes of their time together flitted through her brain. She recalled all the wonderful, caring things Russ had done for her.

He'd demonstrated his dependability. Shown how fiercely he protected those in need. How much he cared about doing the right thing and behaving honorably. How tough, yet gentle he could be.

How had she let a man who clearly didn't want the responsibility of raising a teenager get to her when she'd sworn not to?

It really didn't matter. Not in the long run. He was so mad at her for not telling him about the loss of her gun that she doubted she'd see him again unless he came back to arrest her. She'd simply followed Sarge's orders. Now it looked as if she'd take the fall for killing Dixon.

Weary, Russ swiveled his chair away from his desk. As the chief of police, he was in a precarious position. He owed it to the townspeople to keep an eye on Sydney in case she took off, but personally, he was more concerned for her safety. As mad as he was at her for not telling him about her gun, when she fixed her pain-filled gaze on him, it was all he could do to keep walking.

He knew she didn't kill Dixon and shouldn't have been so rough on her. The only thing she was guilty of was leaving her gun in the car. Not something worthy of arrest.

Oh, but he knew from experience it *was* something she could catch blame for. Blame that could ruin her life if she let it. Like he had his. Instead of helping her deal with the gut-wrenching pain he'd yelled at her, making things worse.

He slammed a fist on the arm of his chair. Sure, he was miffed that she hadn't told him about the missing weapon, but that wasn't reason to go off on her like that. What he should've done was shout at himself for daring to care about a woman again. After all, that was why he was so mad, wasn't it? He'd opened his heart to her only to find out it didn't pay off.

What he wouldn't give right now to go back to the way things were before he'd dared to hope. Maybe she was thinking the same thing. Wishing she'd never run into him again. Feeling the same turmoil.

At least she had God to turn to. He did, too, if he'd only try.

He closed his eyes and fought for the words he needed to convey his thoughts to God, but they tangled. He couldn't think clearly. The pressure to ask for the right thing was nearly palpable. Then he remembered what Reid had once taught him. When you don't know what to pray for, God still knows your needs.

Well, then, God. If Reid is right, You know what

*I need. Please bring it to pass, because I'm at the
end of my rope and the killer is inching closer to
Sydney.*

"Ah, Chief?" Garber said from the door of the
office, drawing Russ's head up.

"What is it?" Russ couldn't believe how weary
his voice sounded.

"Got the info back from the building inspector. He
says the invoices on Dixon's computer don't match
the materials in the photos. Looks like Johnson installed substandard products and turned in invoices
to the construction company for higher-grade items,
then pocketed the difference."

Maybe they finally had a real suspect. "We need
to get Johnson's bank statements."

"Way ahead of you. He's been making regular
cash deposits well above his salary. A few months
ago, he also started taking hefty withdrawals. I
figure that money was paying off Dixon."

"And then he got tired of being blackmailed and
killed him."

Garber nodded. "He probably knew Deputy
Tucker stopped at the town houses every night and
had heard she'd threatened Dixon. He swiped her
gun and killed Dixon, then was going to kill her,
making it look like a murder-suicide, but you showed
up."

"Makes sense. But how does that explain the
texts?"

"Could be plan B. When he didn't take Tucker out,

he decided to make it look like she took this mystery item to make us question if she was involved with Dixon. Then all he had to do was leave her gun for us to find and hope circumstantial evidence convicted her."

"Sounds possible," Russ said. "Let's bring Johnson in and start tracking down his whereabouts at the time of the murder and the other incidents."

Baker poked his head in the door and handed Russ a sheet of paper. "Ballistics."

Russ took the page, but before looking at it he dismissed his men. No way he'd let them see his reaction to the report's contents.

When both officers exited, Russ laid the paper on top of his desk. Though he believed with all his heart in Sydney's innocence, he couldn't bring himself to look at the report. He sat staring, but unseeing as time passed.

"Chief," Garber said from the door. "We've located Johnson. Should have him here within thirty minutes."

"Let me know when he gets here."

"You okay, boss?"

"Fine," he answered.

"Was it Deputy Tucker's gun?"

Russ couldn't put off looking any longer or Garber would start to question his tactics. He peered at the report. What he'd dreaded had come to pass. Sydney's gun killed Dixon.

"Yeah, it's hers."

"Want me to bring her in?"

Should he? If the report confirmed a gun belonging to anyone other than Sydney or maybe other than another law-enforcement officer, he'd be out the door and on his way to get an arrest warrant. But this was Sydney. A fellow officer of the law.

So how did he handle this? He could call Reid for advice, but this was Russ's responsibility. He needed to step up and decide what to do on his own.

"Chief?"

"I'm really not liking her for this, Garber. Let's wait to do anything until after we talk with Johnson."

"You got it. I'll let you know when Johnson arrives." Garber departed and Russ went to the window.

The overcast sky blocking the sunlight reflected his mood. Was he doing the right thing here? Or was he letting feelings for Sydney obscure his judgment just like the thick clouds blocked the sun?

"I'm surprised to find you standing here when there's an arrest to be made," Windsor said from behind.

Russ turned, spotting the councilman leaning on the doorjamb, his thick arms crossed. How Windsor had heard the news so fast was beyond Russ.

"We just got the report. Give me time to process the news."

"Why? Because she's a deputy and law-enforcement officers stick together?" Windsor pushed off the door and came into the room.

"No, because I think we have other suspects to consider first."

"That may be the case, but there's sufficient evidence to arrest her and we don't want her fleeing while you dawdle," Windsor said curtly.

"Circumstantial evidence that I'm not sure a judge will issue a warrant for."

"I'm way ahead of you there. You do the paperwork...I'll make sure it gets signed."

Russ clamped his hand on his gun and looked at Windsor. "No one is going to push me into this."

"You like your job, don't you?" Windsor adopted a haughty look.

"You know I do."

"Then I suggest you make the arrest or you'll find yourself unemployed and without a reference to find another job." He walked to the door and looked at his watch. "I'll give you until ten o'clock to bring me the paperwork. If you don't want to comply, start packing your things."

Russ fumed inside but kept his expression blank so Windsor didn't find any satisfaction over riling him. When the councilman was out of sight, Russ dropped onto his chair. He wouldn't let anyone push him around. He was an officer of the law. He'd abide by the oath he'd sworn to uphold.

Trouble was, he didn't know if he could make the right move here. This job was everything to him. If he disobeyed this direct order from Windsor, with his past problem with alcohol, he'd never find another job in law enforcement. But that wasn't reason enough to arrest Sydney. Not if he wasn't convinced of her guilt.

His head felt as if it would explode from indecision. For the first time in his professional career, he felt paralyzed. If he didn't find a way to work through it, the paralysis could cost someone their life.

SIXTEEN

Sydney didn't think she could handle another person disappointed in her, but she didn't want Sarge to hear the news about her gun from someone else so she'd phoned him. He exploded, letting his voice travel through the line and reverberate around the cabin.

She stood by, letting him get it all out. She deserved every bit of his wrath.

"I'm coming out there," he said, his tone calm and measured. "We need to figure out a way to spin this before your carelessness tarnishes every member of the sheriff's department. I'm just down the road and will be there in a few minutes." He disconnected before she could argue.

Before she could stow her phone, it rang. Expecting a return call from Sarge saying something had come up and he couldn't make it, she dug out the phone and glanced at caller ID.

Not Sarge, but Reid.

Was there a security breach? Or maybe this was about Nikki.

Sydney clicked talk. "What's wrong, Reid?"

"I hate to tell you this." He paused, the silence long and painful. "Nikki's missing."

"Missing? What do you mean missing?" Distress brought a lump to her throat.

"Before you panic, there's no sign of forced entry or a struggle, so we don't think she's been abducted. My men thought she was sleeping, but when she didn't come out, they were worried and checked on her. Found the window unlocked and her gone. Looks like she simply decided to split."

"She doesn't know anyone in Portland. So where would she go?"

"Maybe she met someone online."

"Possible." Sydney tried to get inside Nikki's head, a challenge to do with a teenager. "Since it's Saturday, she might've called her friend Emily to give her a ride back home."

"Can you check with Emily and get back to me?"

"Sure." She disconnected and made a quick call to Nikki first, just in case she answered.

Five rings. Voice mail. She left a message to call ASAP, then dialed Emily. No answer. Sydney located Emily's home number in her phone book.

When Emily's mother answered, Sydney explained her problem, minus all of the details about the killer. Ann went to see if Emily was in her room. As Sydney waited for her to return, she tapped her foot on the floor.

If Nikki wasn't with Emily, Sydney would need to

go look for her. But where did she start? She didn't have a clue where her sister would go in Portland. But the killer might. He could've followed her. Or Reid could be wrong and the killer had already abducted Nikki.

In that case, baiting the killer to draw him away from Nikki was Sydney's best option. Actually, the best option in either case. The very thing Russ and Reid warned her not to do. Too bad, because Nikki came first. She always came first.

"Sydney." Ann's soft voice came over the phone. "Emily's here like I thought. She says she hasn't heard from Nikki since that dreadful party the other night."

"Thanks, Ann."

"Can I—"

Sydney clicked off before Ann asked for details Sydney wasn't willing or able to share.

Trying to come up with a plan, she paced the room until she heard Claudia's phone ring from the porch. Maybe something else was going down. Something Reid didn't want to tell her about. Could be news on Nikki.

Sydney went to the door and stepped into the cold. Her breath fanned out in airy wisps as she crossed the porch to Claudia.

"Everything okay?" the other woman asked.

"Was that call about Nikki?"

"It was Reid telling me your sergeant is on his way up here." She nodded toward his cruiser creeping up the far end of the driveway. "You're not planning on leaving with him, are you?"

"What?"

"I know you're itching to get out of here, but I wouldn't recommend leaving," she said, her expression concerned. "In fact, I'm dead set against it."

Claudia's warning gave Sydney an idea. She would convince Sarge to let her leave with him and help her find Nikki.

"I don't like that look, Deputy," Claudia said. "Don't do something stupid or I'll have to come after you." She smiled as if this was a joke, but her serious tone told Sydney that if she left the woman would track her down. But that wouldn't stop Sydney.

Trying to figure out how to get Sarge on her side, she waited for him to join them, then introduced him to Claudia.

He gave the former agent a clipped nod and jerked his head at the door. "Inside, Tucker. Now!"

"Remember what I said, Deputy," Claudia called after them.

Sarge raised an eyebrow in her direction but didn't stop his long strides into the house. Sydney followed him into the living room, where he jabbed a finger at the club chair. She sat. He paced. He always paced. Probably why he resembled a human string bean.

She didn't wait for him to launch into his tirade, but preempted it. "Before we talk about my gun, I have a pressing issue that I need your help with." She explained Nikki's disappearance to Sarge, imbuing her voice with the urgency she felt. "I was hoping you'd take me out of here so I can find her."

He appraised her, his dark eyes settling on her face. "I'm not sure that's such a good idea, Tucker."

"What if one of your family members was missing and a killer was on the loose? What would you do?"

"I'd bust outta here." His lips tipped in a half smile.

"And you'd want some help if it was available, right?"

He sighed with exasperation. "What do you want me to do?"

"I need to hide in your vehicle when you leave."

"Don't know if that'll work, Tucker. Morgan is such a stickler for protocol. He searched my cruiser on the way in and will do it on the way out."

"So what if he does? I'm not a prisoner... I can leave. If Reid follows us, with your stellar driving, you can easily lose him." She really didn't think Sarge could outmaneuver Reid, but Sarge often acted based on his ego, so she shamelessly fed it.

"You got that right." He clamped a hand on his jaw and looked up in his thinking pose. "Okay, this is what we do. I'll go out and offer to spell the agent on the porch."

"Claudia. Her name's Claudia."

"We'll both go outside to talk to *Claudia*. You act all upset, like I really let you have it over your gun—which, by the way, I'm gonna do when this is all over." He pierced her with a hard stare. "Got it?"

"Yes."

"Good. Tell Claudia you're gonna lie down. Go to your room, lock the door. Turn on a TV, radio, whatever's in there to make noise. When Claudia goes inside, I'll keep an eye on her. If she doesn't follow you, I'll call you and you can slip out the window."

"Perfect. Thanks, Sarge. I'll owe you big-time for this."

"Yeah, you will." He went to the door.

She followed and almost called things off when Claudia's gaze expressed continued concern for her safety. Sydney hated to do something so underhanded to the woman, but Nikki needed her, so she moved forward.

Together she and Sarge worked their plan and even though Claudia seemed suspicious, it went off without a hitch. Reid allowed them to pass, and she relaxed as much as one could in the trunk of a car as the tires spun over the highway. They traveled for miles, damp cold seeping into her bones, before Sarge stopped and let her out. She hurried into the passenger seat and turned on the heat.

"Where to?" Sarge asked.

"My house to get my car."

"Then let's not dawdle." He flipped on the lights and siren and shot down the road.

She'd ridden with him before and felt comfortable with his high-speed driving, but today the sun perched at the right spot to send blinding rays through the windshield. She offered a quick prayer for their safety and kept her eyes on the surroundings, making sure the killer wasn't following them.

"Would you mind parking in the alley a few doors down in case the killer is staking out my house?" she asked.

"Not likely he's anywhere around here. He has to know this is the last place you'll come."

"Humor me, okay?"

"Fine." He turned the corner and eased into the alley.

With the sun rapidly descending, deep shadows reflected into the tight space, sending chills over Sydney's arms. Maybe the alley wasn't such a good idea after all.

"So do you have a plan, or are you gonna run off half-cocked?" Sarge asked, shifting into Park.

"I have a plan."

"Want to run it by me?" he said. "I might be able to help."

"You won't try to stop me?"

"No." He turned off the ignition.

She opened her door. "I'll tell you once we get inside so I don't waste time."

They climbed out and quickly walked to her back stoop. Even as she unlocked the door, she kept a vigilant eye on the surroundings, but Sarge must've really believed the killer was nowhere in sight as he relaxed against the wall and waited for her to open the door.

She stepped inside first. The mess left behind

from the invasion tugged out a sigh. But the mess wasn't worth thinking about with her sister missing, so she continued picking her way through her belongings to get to Nikki's room, where she went straight to her computer.

She woke it up. "My gut says the killer couldn't possibly have known the safe-house location and he doesn't have Nikki. After I find her and make sure she's safe, I'll send a text to the killer. Lure him out and away from Nikki."

Sarge stopped next to her. "Okay, first, how are you gonna find her?"

"I'm logging on to our cell provider to see if she made any calls." Sydney clicked away on the keyboard. "Nikki isn't supposed to use her phone right now, but if I know my sister, she called someone. The listing won't include the name or address, but hopefully I can use reverse phone lookup to find it."

"If not, I'll pull a few strings and get the name for you."

"You'd do that?" she asked.

"Why not?"

She glanced up at him. "No offense, Sarge, but you're a by-the-book kinda guy. This is so breaking the rules."

"Sometimes the rules are made to be broken." His face took on a mischievous look. "But don't ever let me catch you breaking them, Tucker."

She didn't know how to react to a side of this

usually strict, no-nonsense man. A man who rarely cracked a smile and held her to high standards.

The screen opened. "She only made one call. Here." She pointed at the listing. "It's a Portland number. I think I've seen it before, but I don't know who it belongs to."

She surfed to a reverse-lookup site and typed in the number. "Unlisted."

"Let me see what I can do." Sarge took out his phone and went in the other room.

He probably didn't want her to hear how he was circumventing procedure to get the number so she couldn't ever duplicate it on the job.

She took the time to open Nikki's email. Until a few months ago, she'd trusted Nikki and never invaded her privacy. But after the problems of late, she'd insisted Nikki remove her screen password so Sydney could access her computer if she wanted. She'd never done so, but counted on the fact that her access might keep Nikki from doing something dumb.

Sydney scrolled down the listings. Nothing since before their trip to the lodge. So it was just the one phone call.

Sarge returned. "Number belongs to a Tara Vincent. Know her?"

Sydney's mouth dropped open.

"Guess that means you do."

Sydney worked hard on curbing her emotions

before answering. "Our mother. She took her maiden name after the divorce."

He held out a small notebook. "I have her address. If you want, I'll go with you to check things out."

Sydney flashed up her hand. "No! This is something I have to do on my own."

Sydney took the paper Sarge ripped from his notebook. She asked him to watch to make sure no one followed her then headed for her car.

Seeing her mother again for the first time in eleven years wasn't something Sydney wanted to do. Not now. Not ever. But leaving Nikki in her mother's clutches wasn't an option.

Dread biting into her heart, she climbed into her cruiser and eased onto the road. She headed for the highway to Portland for the forty-minute drive. She hoped to use the time to prepare herself to see a woman who'd discarded her like trash.

Russ sat on a bench in the courtyard outside his office. Darkness had descended, leaving the area as shadowed as his thoughts. He couldn't come to a decision about Sydney.

He lifted his face to the sky, peppered with twinkling stars. "God, if you're there, please show me what to do."

He propped his elbows on his knees, resting his chin on his hands. A Bible verse came to his mind, as if God were whispering the words in his ear. *And we know that in all things God works for the good of those who love him.*

The same thing Sydney had said to him in the delivery truck. Bad things happen—like losing the job you thrive on or not having a chance with the woman you've come to love—but whatever happened, if he reacted positively to these events, then God could work it for good. And, as Sydney said, he could use what he learned in the hard times to help others. Much like he'd helped Nikki.

So, he could play it safe—arrest Sydney and keep his job—or do what his gut told him was the right thing to do here—find the real killer. He might lose his job but God would see him though whatever occurred. All he had to do was remember that. To call upon God's strength when he felt weak and he could do anything.

Thank You, God, for being here. Thank You for bringing Sydney into my life. Please, Lord, help me to put aside my desire to keep my job. Help me do what's right for her.

"There you are," Reid said, entering the courtyard. "I've been trying to call you."

"I had some thinking to do, so I turned off my phone." Russ pulled his cell out and powered it up. "Wait. What're you doing here? Who's watching Sydney?"

"She took off."

"What?" Russ's raised voice reverberated off the

walls surrounding them and all the trust he'd just placed in God threatened to evaporate.

"I think she's with Krueger," Reid said.

"You think?"

"I'm nearly positive."

"Explain," Russ demanded.

"Earlier this afternoon I called Sydney to tell her Nikki took off."

"Seriously?" Russ jumped to his feet. "A few hours away and everything falls apart. What happened?"

"She was hanging out in her room at the safe house. After a while the guys got worried when she didn't come out, so they went to check on her. The window was unlocked but there was no sign of foul play. We believe she decided to split."

"Just like she did the other night. So what happened with Sydney?"

"She was supposed to check with Nikki's friend to see if Nikki was with her and call me back. When Sydney didn't call back, I called her. She didn't answer." Reid cleared his throat. "Claudia followed up and found Sydney was missing. This was minutes after Krueger came by to talk to Sydney about her gun, so the only logical explanation is she got Krueger to give her a ride."

Russ clamped a hand on his neck and paced. "This is my fault. I yelled at her for not telling me about her gun. Now she probably thinks I won't help her clear her name and she has to do it on her own."

"I think it has more to do with Nikki taking off."

"Maybe. Maybe not." Russ searched for an idea of what to do next. "We need to get into her head and figure out what she's up to."

"Seems like we have two choices here. She went to find Nikki or she's trying to lure out the killer."

"Our best bet is to get the phone company to give us her location by triangulating her cell." Reid dug out his phone. "I'll call my buds at the FBI to get that started."

"That's good, but cutting through the red tape could take hours. I'm not gonna sit here and wait."

"You got a better idea?"

"Not really, but if I was going after a killer I'd want to be prepared. First thing I'd do is head home to get items I'd need to carry out my mission."

"Me, too." Reid stood. "So let's scope out her house, then."

"We need to move fast." Russ's tone filled with heaviness. "This killer is too good. No way a rookie can handle him."

Tossing up a prayer for Sydney's safety, Russ charged toward his cruiser and fired up both siren and lights. Reid climbed in next to him and they raced through the streets of Logan Lake. Reid talked with his buddy Jack Duger, who promised to do his best to obtain her location.

"I only hope the killer hasn't gotten to Sydney first," Reid said after he disconnected.

His brother's tone upped his anxiety level. If that was possible. He hadn't been this frazzled since Willie died.

Okay, God. I'm failing here. I need Your strength to get through this.

There. That should help. He waited for the easing of the knot in his stomach. Didn't happen. He needed to keep his focus on trusting God. Maybe the pain would diminish.

They pulled up to her house.

"Don't see her car." Russ shifted into Park and searched the area.

"She could've parked in the garage." Reid withdrew his gun.

Russ followed suit and grabbed his door handle.

An explosion rocked the car. Sydney's house disappeared in orange-and-blue flames shooting into the air. Debris reined down on them, pinging off the roof. The windshield cracked like thin ice on a pond.

Russ ducked and covered his head. Saw Reid do the same thing.

When the fallout stopped, he raised his head. The structure sizzled and snapped with flames.

"No! Sydney!" He jumped from the car. As he approached the house, heat seared his face and thick smoke clouded his vision. He put an arm up to protect his eyes. A few more steps.

A neighbor rushed up to them. "What happened?"

"Call 911," Reid commanded in a tone that told the man to ask no further questions.

Russ stood, staring. In shock over the sight before him.

Reid eased closer. "We have no proof she's in there, Russ."

"I know. My gut even says I'd know if she was in there, but still…" His words fell off as he imagined a life without Sydney.

Reid turned Russ to face him. "Don't go there, bro. Unless we have confirmation, it's a waste of time." Reid held his hands out. "Look. There's a crowd forming. As police chief, you need to take control of the situation so when the fire department arrives they can do their job."

Russ heard Reid's words, but didn't want to let them register. He was the police chief, all right. It was the job he'd lived for. Until right now. The job meant nothing. Absolutely nothing. It was just a job and wasn't enough for him. Not since Sydney came into his life again. She was so much more than the job. But Reid was right. They had no evidence that she was inside and there was no use letting fear paralyze him, making the situation worse.

Russ turned to the growing crowd and dug to his core to find the strength to do his job. "Okay, people, you need to back up so we can make room for the fire truck."

"Is Sydney okay?" a woman shouted.

"We aren't sure she was home," Russ answered.

"I saw her come home a little while ago, but I didn't see her lea—" The words were torn away on a sob.

"Doesn't look like her car is here, so that's a good sign," Reid said.

"She didn't drive up in her car. She was walking."

Russ shared a look with Reid. Russ didn't try to hide his sorrow. If anyone understood Russ's emotions right now, it was his brother. He knew all about losing the woman he loved.

No. Russ wouldn't think that way. Not until a firefighter confirmed it. He had to keep hoping. Something in his gut told him she was alive. He'd hang on to that for now and do his job.

Uncertain what to do, Sydney stood inside the door of her mother's small bungalow. Nikki held their mother's hand while Sydney let it sink in that after eleven years she was facing the woman who hadn't wanted them. The woman who'd been verbally abusive. The woman who'd ended Sydney's childhood and forced her to take on responsibilities she wasn't ready to assume.

Sydney stared at the wrinkled hand holding Nikki's soft one. She glanced at the aged face, making sure not to linger in her eyes filled with hope. Alcohol abuse had aged their mother beyond her years. She claimed she'd quit drinking. Been sober for a few years now, she said. That's why she contacted them. Wanted their forgiveness. But a ten-minute conversation wasn't enough to let Sydney forgive years' worth of hurt.

"Sydney," her mother said. "Please don't go. Sit down. Let's talk."

"I can't. C'mon, Nikki…we're leaving."

"But it's not safe out there."

"And it's not safe here. It won't take long for someone to find Mom's address and come looking for us."

"Then she should come with us, too," Nikki insisted.

"I'll arrange for her to go to the safe house."

"I'll go with her."

"No!" Sydney regretted her outburst the moment it happened. "I'm sorry, Nikki, but I need you to come with me. When this is all over, we'll all sit down and have a talk."

"You promise?"

"Yes, I promise," she said, giving her sister a look that ensured she would keep her word.

"Okay." Nikki got up, hugged their mother and crossed the room.

Sydney looked at her mother. "Pack a bag. The FBI agents will be here soon to move you someplace safe."

"It was good to see you, Sydney. I look forward to seeing you again." Her tone was hopeful, but still that of a stranger.

Sydney left the house and surveyed the street before easing Nikki out the door behind her. She opened the passenger door and waited for Nikki to settle, then ran around the front of the car and got in.

Distracted by seeing her mother, Sydney was lucky she navigated safely through the streets. At the first stop sign, she sighed out her tension and ran her hands through her hair, stopping to massage a tight muscle at the base of her skull.

"How odd," a male voice said from the backseat. "I have a headache, too."

Nikki screamed and Sydney spun around. A gun pointed at them through the metal grille separating the seats.

"Hello, Deputy Tucker." The large man grinned. "Pull into a parking space."

She did as told, then shifted in her seat to get a good look at the man. A man she'd never seen before. He had a long face, covered with stubble that matched salt-and-pepper hair cut short. Powerfully built, he sported a large tattoo of a snake on the arm raised with the gun.

He let out a coarse laugh. "If you're finished studying me, I suggest we proceed."

"What do you want?"

His expression sobered. "We want the flash drive you took from Dixon's house."

We? So there was more than one person involved in this. "Who are you working with?"

"You'll find that out in due time. But first, the flash drive."

"I didn't take a flash drive."

He tsked. "I'd so hoped you'd cooperate with me, but I guess we'll have to do this the hard way. Now do be a good girl, turn around and place your hands on the wheel where I can see them."

Frantically searching for a way out of this situation, she turned and laid her hands on the wheel. Maybe if she kept him talking they could escape. Complimenting him on his prowess was a good place to start.

"You know, I'm impressed. Despite all of our precautions, you always manage to find me. How do you do it?"

He chuckled. "A sweet little program downloaded onto your phone when you were up on the hill. It lets me listen in to your calls. Even turn on the speaker whenever I want to see what you're up to."

Why didn't she think of this? Spyware for cell phones had been in the news lately. She'd read all about it.

"That when you took my gun, too?"

"Yes, of course. You really should be more careful with your weapons. Now enough of this chatter. It's time to go." His forceful tone sent chills up her spine. "I'm going to slide a blindfold through the grille, Nikki. Tie it tightly in place, then put your hands on the dashboard."

Nikki shot Sydney a plea to help her but complied.

Sydney wanted to rip her hands from the wheel, spin and slam the gun into this man's face. But she knew better. Knew he'd fire a shot at Nikki before she could do anything.

"Good," he said. "Now your turn, Deputy."

She felt the cloth of the blindfold brush against her neck and over her shoulder. She resisted the urge to grab it and toss it to the floor. As much as she didn't want to, she had to comply with this thug's demands until she could gain the upper hand.

Something she had to do, and soon. He'd let them see his face. That meant only one thing. No matter what happened, he planned to kill them both.

SEVENTEEN

In the trunk of her car, Sydney shifted into a more comfortable position, if such a position existed with her hands cuffed behind her back and a gag in her mouth. The guy had dragged them out of the car and slapped cuffs on their wrists. He'd searched her for a weapon and her cell phone. Thankfully, she'd dropped it into her backpack, which she'd tossed on the backseat.

The car slowed and rumbled over ruts as if they navigated a rough driveway. She felt the car wind down a hill, causing her to roll toward the back of the trunk and Nikki to slam into her. They came to a stop. Mere seconds later he hauled out Nikki and slammed the trunk closed.

Panic settled over Sydney like a wet blanket, stealing her breath and speeding her heart.

Lord, please don't let him hurt Nikki. If anyone has to get hurt let it be me.

Blood pounding in her ears, she listened, hoping to hear footsteps returning for her. It wasn't long before her wish came true. Except the trunk didn't open and the car started moving again. He was separating her from Nikki. A smart move for the killer, not a good thing for them.

When the car hit the main road again, Sydney decided to count and pay attention to turns so she knew how far away he was taking her from Nikki. Two turns, both rights, and about fifteen minutes later, they arrived at another location. She braced herself for what was to come.

The trunk opened and her captor jerked her out. She struggled against arms of steel clamped around her chest. This maniac held her so tightly she could hardly breathe.

He dragged her across a yard, up a short flight of stairs and over a threshold. He slammed her down onto a wooden chair and held fast until he'd secured a rope around her chest. Then he bound her legs and finally wound a rope around her stomach.

She felt him checking the knots, tugging them tight.

She groaned, but her cries didn't seem to affect him. He jerked off her blindfold and marched back outside. As her eyes adjusted to the light from the bare bulb hanging from the ceiling, she shifted, testing the ropes and trying to loosen them. Her only hope to get free was to find something to slice through them. She searched the small cabin undergoing renovation. A tiny kitchenette was to her back and a combo family room and dining space to her side.

Her captor's footfalls came back up the steps. She stilled. He dropped her backpack on the floor near the door. "Wouldn't do to get caught with this in the car."

Odd. Was he planning to leave her here? But why?

He crossed the room, retrieved a tote bag from a worn plaid sofa and gently set it on the floor next to her chair. He slid the long zipper back and reached into the bag with both hands.

As she waited to see what he withdrew, her heart raced. He lifted his hands, cautiously extracting something between the zippers.

She gasped.

A bomb. He was holding a bomb. It looked like the fake one tossed through the window at the lodge. He rose and looked down on her, a sick smile on his face. She squirmed. Screamed against the gag.

"I told you the next one would be real," he said. "I'm going to strap this to your chest. It has a motion sensor. Once I activate it if you move more than a few inches it'll be the last thing you do. Nod if you understand me."

She nodded and he strapped on the bomb. Finished, he activated it and held up a small remote. "FYI, I can also detonate it with this, too."

Fear and panic beyond anything she'd ever known slithered over her skin and settled into her stomach. She tried not to let the fear show in her eyes, but she was sure she hadn't controlled it.

"This will give you some time to think about turning over the drive." He spun on his heels. At the doorway, he stopped. "Unless, of course, you want to tell me where it is now."

She shook her head. Even if she did have it, once she gave it to him he'd detonate the bomb.

"You've proven to be very resourceful, Deputy. In case you figure out a way to leave, I suggest you think twice, as your sister is wearing an identical device. Wouldn't want her to get hurt, now would we?" Another sick grin and he flipped off the lights and closed the door.

Darkness descended, surrounding her with terror. No one but Sarge knew where she'd gone. Even if Russ or Reid got Sarge to tell them about her mother's house, which she doubted Sarge would do, that information wouldn't lead them to this cabin. She and Nikki were on their own. Nothing short of a miracle could save them now.

Russ wanted to do something, anything, but watching the firefighters battle the blaze consumed his thoughts. His little brother, Ryan, a volunteer firefighter for the past few years, looked back at Russ, but his face shield hid his eyes. When Ryan had arrived, his face declared if Sydney was in the house, there was no hope for her. Not that he'd needed Ryan to confirm it.

Russ was doing a great job of imagining the flash of surprise on Sydney's face when the bomb exploded. He couldn't imagine what happened next. That would be too horrible.

"Hey, bro," Reid called out as he crossed the street. "Sydney's cell phone is transmitting a signal."

A glimmer of hope flickered to life. "A cell wouldn't operate in that house."

"Exactly." Reid smiled. "The triangulated location shows the signal moving up the highway leaving Portland and heading east. We have the phone company on standby. They're pinging her phone so we can tail her. Last ping puts her thirty minutes out."

"Let's go. We'll push it. Get to her in twenty." Russ took off for his car, winding though the spectators. Not stopping to apologize when he bumped into them.

At the car, Reid jerked him to a stop. "Let's think this through before racing off. Sydney may not have her phone with her. The killer could've taken it so she wasn't able to call for help."

"Either way, we need to follow this lead. If she's in possession of the phone, she could need our help." Russ's voice trembled. "If he took her phone, we need to bring him in."

"You're too emotionally involved to make that arrest."

"You're probably right, but I won't stand around here and wait for Ryan to tell me they found a body in the house." Russ shrugged off Reid's hand. "You can come with me, but don't try to stop me."

Russ climbed in and his brother followed suit. Russ wasn't sure if he wanted his brother to accompany him. If Russ found the killer in the possession of Sydney's cell, who knew what he might do?

Russ drove, his mind focused on the road and getting to Sydney as fast as possible, while Reid consulted on speakerphone with his FBI buddy Jack Duger. About twenty minutes ago, the signal had stopped moving. Russ hoped to catch up to Sydney in a few more minutes.

"Take a left about a mile ahead." Reid relayed the road name. "A few more miles will put you on a hill overlooking the property."

"How about the terrain?" Russ asked.

"I'm emailing the satellite image now," Duger answered on speakerphone. "It'll be hard to view on a cell so let me run down the topography." He described the hilly terrain, the dense trees and layout of the lot.

Reid pointed ahead on the road. "That's our turn."

"I'll let you know as soon as we have anything else," Duger said.

"Thanks, buddy," Reid replied. "Would appreciate it if you'd request backup."

"You got it. Good luck."

Russ came to a stop at the side of the road. They silently climbed out, located night-vision goggles and binoculars from the trunk, then knelt in the dirt to search the area. If Sydney was in that cabin, there was no sign of her.

No car. No lights. No person.

"I don't know, bro," Russ said. "Something isn't right."

"Agreed," Reid answered. "But these are the right coordinates. Maybe the killer drove out here to ditch her phone and lead us down a dead end."

"Only one way to find out. I'm going down there." Russ rose to his feet. "You maintain surveillance. Call me if there's anything I need to know." Russ didn't give Reid a chance to stop him but eased into the scrub.

He picked his way through dense brush. Even with goggles showing the way, branches clawed at his body, slapping his face. He didn't care. He had to find Sydney. Alive. He kept going, one foot in front of the other, until he broke into the clearing.

He phoned Reid. "I'm near the cabin. Anything I need to know?"

"You're clear. I'll cover you."

Russ stowed his phone. As quietly as possible, he jimmied the lock on a window and climbed in. He slipped through the house, searching through the goggles' colored lenses. In the front room, he spotted a woman. From behind, he wasn't sure of her ID, but she was roped to a chair so he had to assume it was Sydney.

He wanted to race into the room, drag her into his arms, but this was exactly the kind of mistake Russ couldn't afford to make. He couldn't let emotions usurp common sense. Breath held, he searched all the rooms.

She was alone. Not a very smart move on the killer's part, but a break for Russ. He returned to the main room.

"Sydney," he said, his voice low to keep from startling her. "Are you alone?"

She nodded, but said nothing. He flipped on his Maglite and lifted the goggles as he rounded her chair.

He sucked in a deep breath. Thought his heart might stop beating. A bomb strapped to her chest rose and fell with her breathing. Her terrified eyes were wide; a drab scarf circled her mouth.

He lifted a hand. Let it fall. Could he touch her or would that set off the bomb?

"You think it's safe to remove your gag?" he asked.

She gave a slight nod.

He went to the wall and switched on the light, returned and gently untied the scarf. She gagged as he withdrew it.

"Thank God you found me." Her voice was dry, raspy. "After our argument I didn't know if you would look for me."

Her comment cut him to the core. He only hoped he could undo the damage his rash behavior had caused.

"I'm sorry for everything I said, Syd. You did the right thing listening to Krueger about the gun. I was out of line." He knelt on the floor, gently stroking her arm. "I care far too much about you to let a silly disagreement come between us."

"That's what I hoped for, prayed for, even, as I sat here in the dark listening to every sound, waiting to be blown apart." Her face constricted as if reliving the experience.

He wanted to hold her, to promise she'd never be hurt again, but the bomb stood between them.

"Let's get you out of here." He reached out to untie her ropes.

"No! Don't do anything else. The bomb has a motion sensor on it. It'll go off if I move more than a few inches. Plus there's a remote detonator." Panic filled her eyes. "And the killer has Nikki with another bomb. He split us up. Dropped me off here then took off."

Russ fought to stay calm. To ask the right questions. "How did he manage to abduct both of you?"

"It's my fault. When Sarge came to Claudia's, I convinced him to give me a ride home so I could find Nikki. I checked her phone log. She called Mom. I figured since she lived a mile or so from the safe house, that's where Nikki went. So I went there to bring her back to my office for safety." Her voice shook. "When we got in the car, he was waiting for us. He demanded I give him a flash drive he claimed I took from Dixon's house."

"All of this is about a flash drive?"

She nodded. "I've been thinking about what must

be on it. My best guess says it has something that can lead us to Dixon's superiors."

"And that means very dangerous men are after you." Russ exhaled and thought about what to do next. "Our best bet is to find the thug who took you. Can you identify him?"

"I don't know him. I can give you a description, but he's not the only one involved. He mentioned another man. Said I'd find out about him soon enough."

"Let's get Reid in on this. He's up the hill." Russ jerked his phone from the holder and pressed the speaker button. Using a professional tone that wouldn't amp up Sydney's fear, Russ told his brother about the bomb and Nikki. "We need the bomb squad and a team to locate Nikki." He paused and looked at Sydney. "Any idea of Nikki's location?"

"Sort of. She's about fifteen minutes away. Take a left out of the driveway, then drive for about ten minutes until you come to a big hill. Then take another left. I can't tell you the speed we were going so I know this isn't very accurate, but it's the best I could do."

"What about issuing an APB for our suspect?" Reid asked. "He should be easy to spot in Sydney's car."

"No!" Sydney shouted.

"He has a remote detonator." Russ kept his tone calm. "If we try to take him, he might use it. We're better off waiting until this bomb is defused."

Reid promised to arrange the necessary resources and keep Russ updated before he clicked off.

Russ stowed his phone, keeping his eyes on Sydney. He couldn't imagine how she felt with enough C4 strapped to her chest to take out this cabin and the surrounding area. He felt as helpless as he had when he'd approached her house and it exploded. Her house. He had to tell her about that.

"There's something else I need to tell you." When he finished filling her in about the explosion, she didn't say anything but began to shiver.

"Don't, Syd." He softly stroked her knee.

"I know I should be strong, but honestly, the academy didn't prepare me for any of this."

"Nothing could. But it'll be okay. I promise." He didn't know how he could make such a statement when so many things could still go wrong, but he couldn't stand to see her suffer any longer.

She took several deep breaths and sighed. "You need to leave in case this thing goes off."

"I won't leave you, Syd."

"Please. I can't relax if you're in danger."

He laughed and scooted closer to her. "I'm pretty sure you won't relax even if I leave you alone."

"You know what I mean. I can get through this if it's just me, but it's almost like I can't breathe when someone I care about is threatened."

Their eyes met. He could see the fear lodged in hers. Fear for him, if he could believe what she'd said, but did he deserve to have this fabulous woman care for him?

The bomb made a loud clicking noise, sending panic through his heart. Homemade bombs malfunctioned all the time. He had to get her out of here before this thing went off.

He gave her hand a final squeeze and stood to pace and think. His cell rang. He snatched it, hoping Reid was calling to tell him the bomb squad was on their way.

"Someone's turning into the driveway." Reid's words rushed out. "None of our guys are on scene yet, so it has to be the suspect. You need to get out of there."

"I can't leave Sydney."

"If you don't turn off that light and leave, you may spook this guy. He'll trigger the remote."

Russ knew Reid was right, but he hated every bit of it. Telling Sydney what was going on, he jogged across the room and flipped off the light switch. He retrieved his goggles and found his way to her with his Maglite.

"I won't let anything happen to you," he whispered and ran a hand over her soft hair. He bent lower and found her lips, letting his feelings for her transfer through his kiss.

She responded then pulled away. "You have to go."

"I don't want to leave you."

"You have to. I'll be fine."

"I love you, Syd." He retied her gag so the killer didn't know he'd been there.

Hands shaking with frustration, he turned off his light, lowered the goggles and exited the way he'd come in. He slipped around the side of the cabin. The approaching vehicle was a county cruiser, a male driving. Sydney said the killer had taken her car, so this guy was likely the killer. He pulled a mask down over his face before Russ could get a good look at him.

Odd. Sydney had seen the killer, so why hide his face now?

Russ watched as the guy climbed out and entered the cabin. He didn't have Nikki with him, but she could be in the car. Russ made his way across the grass to check. He searched the vehicle, but didn't find her. He did get a good look at the vehicle's ID though. This was a county vehicle, but it wasn't Sydney's car.

So was this the killer or not? Sydney had said more than one man was involved, so maybe that explained why this guy had put on a mask. Maybe, just maybe, he couldn't trigger the bomb and Russ could take him out. He called Reid to give him the car's ID so he could look in a notebook where Russ kept all local LEOs' car IDs.

"You won't believe this," Reid said. "The car belongs to Krueger."

Stunned, Russ sat back on his haunches. "I can't

begin to figure out how he's involved in this, but my gut says we should try to take him out."

"I'm on my way," Reid answered.

"I'll scope things out so when you get down here we can act." Russ circled the building until he could get a clear view through the family-room window. Krueger, if indeed it was him under the mask, stood over Sydney. His mouth moved and Russ could make out garbled conversation.

The good news was Krueger didn't have his gun drawn. The bomb must've made him overconfident.

Russ made his way to the other side of the cabin and told Reid what he'd seen. They planned a strategy. Russ would reenter from the rear and get into position to take a shot at Krueger. Reid would force open the front door, drawing Krueger's attention. Russ would either charge Krueger or shoot him, depending on how Krueger reacted.

Russ started to move into position and heard Krueger badgering Sydney for the flash drive. At least he thought it was Krueger. He had the right build, but he was using the same creepy voice the man had used at the town houses. Russ's finger itched to take him out and end this, but he had to work the plan.

Phone still in his pocket, Russ pressed Send on a call he'd dialed to Reid before entering the cabin. This was the signal for Reid to break in the door.

And he did. Slammed it into the wall, then took cover. Krueger spun, drawing his gun as he went.

Russ charged from his spot and tackled Krueger. The man was as tall as a tree, but the desire to protect Sydney gave Russ superhuman strength.

"Enough, Krueger," Reid called from above them.

This was enough to sidetrack Krueger. Russ overpowered and cuffed him.

As Reid flipped on the light, Russ rolled him over and ripped off his mask. It was Krueger all right. A snarly, angry Krueger.

Reid crossed the room and removed Sydney's gag. "I'll go wait for the bomb squad."

"Thanks," Russ said.

"Why, Sarge?" Sydney asked, her voice raspy. "Why are you doing all of this?"

Krueger opened his mouth, but before he said anything to compromise the case, Russ read him his Miranda rights. Krueger clamped his mouth shut. Fine. They'd get the details out of him later. Russ searched Krueger, as he knew he'd have one or more backup guns. He jerked the growling man to a sitting position.

Krueger broke free and grabbed the leg of Sydney's chair. "Let me go or I'll dump her to the floor."

"You don't want to end your own life," Russ said, though he saw imbalance and rage in Krueger's eyes.

"Would be better than going to jail. Now take off these cuffs and back off."

"Then what? You escape. If my brother doesn't plug you when you step outside, I'll hunt you down. And you know I'll get you."

"Let me worry about that." He lifted his hands a fraction. "The cuffs."

Russ needed to stall. He'd start Krueger talking about his role in this fiasco as a distraction while Russ figured out how to end this.

Slowly, with his hands raised so Krueger didn't overreact and move Sydney, Russ eased toward the tainted cop. "I don't get it, Krueger. Who got you involved in all of this anyway?"

"Involved? You think I'm merely involved?" His voice rose in disbelief before he laughed. It came out maniacal. "I'm the mastermind, you fool. I've run a drug operation in the county for six years. Right under every LEO's nose."

Though appalled, Russ was also impressed that he'd pulled this off for so long. That meant Krueger was a more dangerous foe than Russ thought. "But Dixon was your downfall."

"If I'd been in town, Tucker wouldn't have arrested him and none of this would've happened." He jerked his head toward the cuffs. "Off. Now, Morgan! I mean it."

Russ dropped to his knees and used his eyes to urge Sydney to keep Krueger talking.

"But you made a big mistake," she said, drawing up Krueger's head. "I don't have the flash drive you're looking for. Why would you think I'd take it, anyway?"

"Dixon said you did."

She snorted. "And you believed him?"

"He claimed it holds pictures of your sister buying and using drugs. That when you arrested him, you palmed it so she wouldn't get in trouble."

"Not hardly," Sydney said.

"But that's not the reason you want the drive, is it?" Russ slipped the key into the lock.

"Dixon knew his…ah…usefulness to the organization had come to an end. So he took pictures of my suppliers as an insurance policy. But one of them saw him. Ratted him out. When he couldn't produce the drive, he claimed you had it."

"So you killed him and came after me." She looked at him with rage burning in her eyes.

Russ removed the cuffs.

"And now I'll be leaving." Krueger came to his feet. "Give me your gun. Get mine, as well. And don't forget your backup gun."

Officer training dictated never to give up a weapon, but Russ couldn't see a way out of this situation without complying. So he did.

"The mighty Morgan failing." Krueger stared, his eyes hot and angry. "This's just icing on the cake." One at a time he tucked the guns in his belt with his free hand. Then got to his feet, keeping a hand on the chair at all times.

"Now what?" Russ asked. "Once you step out that

door, I'll be on you. Or Reid or the bomb squad will. You can't go anywhere, so give it up."

"I'm not going alone. I'm taking Tucker with me." He wrapped his foot through the rung on the chair and opened the timing mechanism. "With this dismantled, she'll travel quite nicely."

Sydney locked eyes with Russ. He expected to see fear, terror, but fury filled her eyes. Good. If Krueger somehow got away with her, this determination would keep her alive. But Russ was going to do his best to stop that from happening.

"A few more to go." Krueger removed a wire from the post, slipped his leg from the chair and retrieved his gun, which he pressed to Sydney's temple. He moved the last wire, then stepped to her side.

"You," he said to Russ. "Untie her."

Russ did as instructed. Then Krueger lifted Sydney. She wobbled, looking as if she was going to keel over. Russ wanted to reach out to her. But the last thing she needed was for Krueger to know he had feelings for her. That would only incite him more.

She shook her arms and regained her balance.

"Good," Krueger said. "We'll be leaving, then." He prodded Sydney out the door.

"Everyone back off or Tucker gets it," Krueger yelled.

Russ had no intention of backing off. He followed the madman outside as he tugged Sydney down the stairs.

She glanced back and cut her eyes to the side at construction scaffolding clinging to the porch. Krueger walked on that side. He took her signal to mean she would elbow him into the bars. Tangle him up and end this.

Not a good plan. Too risky. He shook his head.

Too late. She'd turned back.

Russ saw her raise her arm and heave her body into Krueger. A shot rang out. Krueger crashed into the pipes. The scaffolding shivered, groaning as it moved.

Russ raced forward. Dived for Sydney. Came up short.

Iron and wooden planks tumbled to the ground like a house made of cards raining down on Krueger and Sydney. The crash was deafening, robbing Russ of all sanity.

"Nooo!" His keening voice cut through the inky blackness when he saw Sydney's twisted body in the wreckage, blood gushing from her neck.

As he got to his feet and searched for something to use to stem the bleeding, a prayer welled up in his heart. Exploded in his head. He ripped off his shirt and fell to his knees.

There was so much blood. Too much. He balled his shirt and pressed it against her neck. Panic turned his hands cold. His heart filled with icy fear.

Please, God, don't let Sydney die. Not now. Not after I just found her.

EIGHTEEN

A steady beeping sound drew Sydney from sleep. Listening to hushed voices, she opened her eyes. A hospital room? She explored bandages circling her neck and head, and struggled to remember what'd happened.

"She's awake," she heard Russ say from above.

She blinked hard, trying to clear her vision, and felt the warmth of his hand cupping hers. She squeezed and attempted to sit up, but pain and a swirl of dizziness held her to the pillow. She closed her eyes. Felt sleep pulling her back.

"Syd." Russ bent close, his face filling her line of sight. "Don't go back to sleep. I've waited too long for you to wake up to let you leave me again." He turned, worry etching his forehead. "I think you should get the nurse."

"You got it," Reid said and leaned over her. "Welcome back, Sydney. You nearly scared this big old lunk to death." He leaned closer and whispered, "Go easy on him, Syd. It's been a long time since he opened his heart. He's scared to death."

He clapped Russ's back. "Be right back."

Sydney couldn't comprehend what Reid meant, so she looked around the room. "How long have I been here?"

"We're going on day three."

"No wonder I feel so bad." She smiled, but a stab of pain stopped it from widening. "My head hurts."

"The scaffolding landed on your head, leaving you with brain swelling. You also suffered a gunshot wound to the neck. Nearly bled out."

The terrifying events flashed back into her head.

"I've been praying nonstop." He squeezed his eyes closed then reopened them as if the same memories assaulted him. "God got us through this, Syd, and I now know I need Him in my life every day, not just when things are falling apart around me." He squeezed her hand. "And you'll never guess who prayed right along with me."

"Who?"

"Nikki. Can you believe that?"

She shot up. "Nikki? How's Nikki?"

"She's fine."

She clutched Russ's shirt to keep the dizziness at bay. "You're not just saying that?"

"No. She's in the lounge. Been here all three days. I'll get her if you want."

"Please." She slowly lowered her head to the pillow. Russ left and Sydney closed her eyes, replaying the events of Sarge's betrayal. It was hard enough to have been the target of a maniac, but then to learn she'd worked alongside the man every day was nearly too much to handle.

She heard the door open.

"Hey, Nikki," she greeted her sister. The teen raced into the room, followed by Russ and someone dawdling behind that Sydney couldn't make out.

Nikki sat on the side of the bed and grinned. "Wish I could get away with sleeping for three days."

"I'm happy to see you, too." She smiled. "Seriously, that guy didn't hurt you, did he?"

"Nah. I'm fine."

"We found Nikki right after you tackled Krueger." Russ approached the other side of her bed. "She was alone in a cabin. No bomb. Also nabbed the guy working with Krueger. He's agreed to testify against Krueger."

"Guess that means Sarge survived."

"Yeah, but he's going away for a long time." Russ smiled with satisfaction. "We located the flash drive. One of the kids at the party swiped it to use for his homework. He didn't bother to erase the pictures. His teacher saw them and called us. Krueger's suppliers are also now behind bars. And Dixon also lied about having pictures of Nikki on the drive."

"Enough of the business talk," Nikki said. "Someone else's here to see you. She's been sitting with me since the accident." She turned toward the door. "C'mon, Mom."

Sydney's stomach knotted. How could Nikki possibly think she'd want to see their mother?

Nikki got up and twined her fingers through their mother's, drawing her forward. Sydney saw the love and acceptance in Nikki's eyes and wished she could accept her mother as easily. But only raw, aching pain surfaced.

She searched for Russ's hand and held tight. Her time alone in the dark at the cabin had given her a new sense of direction, strengthened her faith, made her realize life was too short not to forgive and give someone a second chance. She should be able to forgive her mother, but even looking at her was proving more difficult than Sydney thought.

She sent a quick, desperate plea to God for help.

"Sydney," her mom said, "I'm glad you're awake. We were worried about you."

"Thank you." Her words were formal. Like a stranger.

Her mother's eyes displayed the hurt. "I shouldn't be here." She backed away.

"No," Nikki said. "You want to talk to her, so do it."

"Is it okay?" she asked Sydney. "Can we talk, or do you want me to leave?"

She really didn't want to talk about this. Not now. Not here. Not ever. But seeing Nikki gazing fondly at their mother reminded Sydney of the promise she'd made to her sister. She'd have to face this at some time, so she might as well get it over with now.

She smiled to reassure her mother. "What did you want to tell me, Mom?"

Her mother drew in a long breath and made solid eye contact. "I'm sorry. Plain and simple. I hurt you beyond measure, and I'm so sorry for what I did." Tears glistened in her mother's eyes. "I could give you all kinds of excuses for my behavior. I could say it was your father's fault for leaving me. But I'm the one who turned to alcohol for comfort. I'm the one who said the horrible things to you. I'm the one who chose to drown my sorrows instead of being the mother you deserved."

Nikki turned to Sydney. "She really is sorry, Syd. She's been sober for two years now."

Her mother nodded. "Two years when I couldn't get up the courage to face you."

"So what's changed?"

"I had a little health scare a month ago and came face-to-face with my mortality."

"You're okay, aren't you?" Nikki asked.

"Fine." Her mother looked lovingly at Nikki. "But it was the wake-up call that I needed. I didn't have forever to talk to you." She stared crying. "And I didn't have forever to spend with you two, to make up for all the things I did wrong or to ask for your forgiveness."

Nikki leaned forward and laid her head on

their mother's shoulder. "You know I forgive you, Mom."

Sydney searched her mother's face for deceit. The pain she found melted Sydney's heart. This was the same look Russ had when he had talked about how he hurt his family—the same sincere remorse mixed with the hope of forgiveness. Russ had messed up in the same way, and Sydney believed with every ounce of her being that he deserved a second chance. Could she do any less with her mother?

No, but the pain and heartache from the years of mistreatment didn't ebb. Letting go of the pain and falling into her mother's arms as easily as Nikki had would take time. But she could offer forgiveness.

"I forgive you, too, Mom," she said softly. "I'd like to spend time with you. See if we can repair our relationship."

Her mother broke into full-out sobs.

Nikki patted her shoulder. "It's okay, Mom. We'll be okay."

Her crying slowed. "Thank you, Sydney. And thank you for bringing Nikki up to be such a fine young woman. I am so proud of both of you."

Nikki offered Sydney an apologetic look. "I'm sorry, too, Syd. I've been making things hard on you. After what Mom told me, I know you were trying to protect me from hearing she wanted to give me away."

A contented sigh slipped out. For once in Sydney's life, she believed everything would be okay.

Nikki would listen more and they would work out how their mother would factor into their lives.

Russ squeezed her hand. She turned to focus on him. Not everything was resolved. She still hadn't told Russ how much he meant to her, and if the anguish in his eyes told her anything, it said he had something to tell her, as well.

She turned back to her mother. "Do you two mind if I talk to Russ for a few minutes?"

"We need to get some lunch." Her mom clearly understood what was going on.

"But I want to talk to Syd," Nikki whined.

"There's plenty of time for that later." Their mother took Nikki's hand and led her out of the room.

Russ perched on the side of the bed, his expression so warm and tender it stole her breath. She sat up, sliding into his arms and resting her head against the warmth of his chest.

He held her so tight breathing was a challenge, but she reveled in the closeness and didn't move. He moved back and leaned down for a kiss. His touch as soft as down and warm as the heat searing her heart.

He suddenly pulled back.

"Why'd you stop?" she asked.

He met her gaze. "I'm so sorry I let this happen to you."

She pulled away. "Oh, no, you don't, Russ. You are not going to take responsibility for this. I was the one who took off on my own. You had nothing to do with that." Vehemence shot through her words.

"Relax, Syd." He stroked her arms. "I'm not blaming myself for this. When I found out you were gone, I did my best to find you and keep you safe. You got hurt. I wish it hadn't happened, but I'm through taking blame for things I can't control."

She sat, openmouthed, for a few moments. "Who are you and where is my Russ?"

His lips tipped in that crooked little grin she loved. "I went to see the Babcocks yesterday. They said if they blamed me for not doing the extra search then they'd have to blame themselves for every little thing that led up to being outside the station when Willie was shot. It helped me realize that although I made a mistake, there were so many other things that day that could've changed the course of events…and that I couldn't continue to blame myself."

She laid a hand on his arm. "I'm so happy to hear that, Russ. You're a terrific guy. You deserve nothing but happiness."

"About that. There's only one way I could be totally happy." He took her hands. "And that's with you by my side. But if you won't consider a future with me, then I have to know it now."

"What? I don't understand. Why wouldn't I consider it?"

He turned the full force of his startling blue eyes on her. "I'm an alcoholic, Syd. I can't promise you I'll never take another drink. I hope and pray that

I won't. I've overcome it so far, but I have to take things as they come."

She squeezed his hand. "If this whole situation taught me anything, it's that *nothing* in our future is certain. We just need to live our lives one day at a time. I'm ready to see where that will take us. Together."

"You also realize I hope to regain partial custody of Zack. Are you prepared to take on a seven-year-old boy?"

"Of course I am. I can't wait to meet your son and get to know him."

"What about Nikki?"

She should've known this was coming...

She dropped his hand. "I won't give her up to be with you, if that's what you're asking."

"What? No. I was going to ask how you think she'll react to us." His eyes narrowed. "Why would you think I'd want you to give her up anyway?"

"Other men have in the past. And you told me that you couldn't raise a teen."

"No, I said I couldn't raise a teenage girl alone like you're doing, but that doesn't mean I wouldn't mind helping you with her." He smiled. "In fact, she's kinda growing on me."

"I'm sorry I jumped to conclusions. Not that it's an excuse, but I've had to go this alone for so long, I'm a little defensive. I'll try to be more trusting."

"And I'll be more patient." He sighed and drew her into his arms.

"You know," she whispered, "we are doing entirely too much talking, Chief Morgan."

"What did you have in mind, Deputy Tucker?"

She tipped her head back and gave him a little pout. "You're the superior officer. I leave that up to you."

"About time you acknowledged my expertise." His mouth crashed down on hers. He deepened the kiss and clutched her tight.

The past few days were worth everything she went through. A few days of pain for a lifetime of happiness—that was quite a bargain.

EPILOGUE

Sydney blew out the candles on the dining table in her new town house and surveyed the room filled with all new belongings. They might have lost everything in the explosion, but now they had a fresh start. Since the construction foreman had been fired for embezzling, it had taken nine long months to finish the project, but she and Nikki were finally settled in.

Russ helped every step of the way, choosing flooring, appliances and fixtures, and the place felt like *their* home. The open space, encompassing a kitchen, family room and dining area with rich wood floors and muted walls, was exactly as she had envisioned. Floor-to-ceiling windows overlooked the moonlit lake, glistening much like the happiness sparkling inside her chest.

She glanced across the room. When she spotted Russ, sitting on the sofa with her Bible in hand, her heart flip-flopped. With Nikki in the picture, she didn't often get a night out with Russ, but once a week they made a point of having dinner alone.

She wasn't going to spend another minute of it cleaning up when she could snuggle up to him on the sofa. When she approached, he set down the Bible and patted the sofa cushion next to him.

He looked confused. "I have another Bible question for you."

"What?" She sat close to him and offered a quick prayer of thanks for the interest Russ had placed on his faith since her rescue.

"I just read in Romans that God works all things for good. Which I can see is true in our situation. Bad things happened to us, but if they hadn't, we wouldn't be together." Russ reached over and lifted her hair over her shoulder. "And finding you is nothing but good."

"So what's the problem?"

"Couldn't God have brought us together in an easier way? Maybe without so much pain along the way?"

She smiled. "Of course He could. But without the pain and suffering, you wouldn't have found your way back to Him. Adversity is often a bridge to God."

"Or away from Him." Russ's pain-filled gaze reminded her how he'd turned to alcohol in his last crisis.

"Yeah, that can happen, too," she said softly and

took his hand. "But fortunately for us, this time you chose the route to God instead of away from Him."

Russ drew her into his arms. "With you by my side, I'll never head in that other direction again."

Happy beyond belief, she snuggled closer.

"Mmm," he whispered. "This's nice. I could really get used to this."

"Why, Chief Morgan." She faked a Southern drawl to lighten the mood and leaned back. "Are you asking me to join forces with you again?"

He smiled back. "Why, yes, I am, Deputy Tucker. I hope this investigation will last for the rest of our lives." He let his finger dip under her chin and slide up and over her lips.

She groaned. "I can't think when you're doing that."

"Mmm," he said and planted kisses on her cheek. "That's the plan."

She put her hands on his shoulders and pushed him back so she could see his face again. "If I tell you that I love you, will you stop tormenting me like this?"

"Why don't you try it and see?"

She laid a hand on the side of his face. "You are perfect for me in so many ways, Russ. I love you." Their eyes connected and an electrical charge passed between them, the current stealing her breath. She could see the same emotion reflected in Russ's eyes, but he nudged her away.

He slid his hand into his pocket and drew out a

shiny ring box. "I've already asked Nikki for your hand, and she's given us her blessing. So all that's left to do is for me to ask and for you to say yes."

Sydney knew she was staring, but she really hadn't expected him to ask her to marry him tonight.

He knelt down on one knee and opened the box. "I love you so much, Syd. Will you marry me?"

"Yes," she breathed.

He slipped the diamond solitaire on her finger and drew her into his arms. He kissed her, infusing it with love.

The sound of a key turning in the door spoiled the mood and they broke apart.

"Nikki," Sydney said, secretly disappointed that their perfect moment had to end.

But Russ didn't seem to mind. Smiling widely, he went to open the door for Nikki.

"You ask her yet?" Nikki asked Russ.

"Yeah, I asked her."

"What she say?" she demanded.

"I'm right here," Sydney said. "You can ask me."

Russ beamed. "She said yes."

"See, I told you she loves you. And you were all worried."

"I wasn't worried."

"You so were." Nikki smirked. "But I don't know why. We both kinda like you."

Russ rubbed his knuckles across Nikki's head. "I love you, too, kid. Now go to your room."

Nikki shot a playful punch to Russ's arm, then

ran across the room and gave Sydney a quick hug. "Thanks for making us a family," she whispered and then shot out of the room.

Russ pulled Sydney close. She snuggled closer, letting her head rest against his chest where he normally wore his badge.

She smiled. At first, she'd only thought of him as a lawman. A strong, capable man who'd committed his life to protecting others, but she'd found so much more. A warm heart, generous spirit, unfaltering devotion. A whole man. The perfect package lay behind the badge and she could ask for nothing more.

* * * * *

Dear Reader,

Thank you for reading Russ and Sydney's story in *Behind the Badge*. This story is special to me, as it is based on the Bible's promise in Romans 8:28— "And we know that in all things God works for the good of those who love Him, who have been called according to His purpose."

Like Sydney and Russ, I have had some tough times in my life. Times when I wondered if God knew what I was going through, and if He did, why didn't He rescue me from these hardships? But when I look back on my difficulties, I can see how God used those trials to make me a better person and to allow me to use what I'd learned in these trials to help others.

How about you? Have you been through the same trials, or maybe you are going through them now?

Your struggle may be like Sydney's, where someone hurt you, disappointed you or failed to follow through on an important promise, causing you pain and anguish. Or maybe you're more like Russ. You did something in your past that you wish you hadn't done and now you struggle with others trusting you or struggle with not believing you should be trusted.

Then you are the person I wrote this book for. Because no matter what has happened in the past, no matter how you feel about the present, one thing is certain: the Lord can and will turn this problem to good.

I pray that the book has encouraged you to trust in the Lord no matter the difficulty you face. I love to hear from readers and you can reach me through my website, www.susansleeman.com, or in care of Love Inspired Books at 233 Broadway, Suite 1001, New York, NY 10279.

Susan Sleeman

QUESTIONS FOR DISCUSSION

1. What is Sydney's biggest challenge as she tries to trust God?

2. What is Russ's biggest challenge? Have you ever experienced something similar?

3. After making a mistake, Russ struggles with worthiness. Have you ever felt as if you weren't worthy because of something you did? If so, how did you overcome it?

4. Why do you think it took Sydney so long to forgive her mother? Have you struggled with forgiving someone? If so, how did you handle it?

5. Which character in the story do you relate most to and why?

6. Sydney and Russ both struggle to trust because of major situations in their lives that seem insurmountable. Do you have issues that keep you from trusting God? If so, what are they?

7. When life was toughest for Russ, he turned to his faith, but as his life settled back down, he slowly let his faith slide. Has that ever happened to you?

8. As the story opens, Russ was in the right place at the right time to save Sydney. Do you think this was coincidence or do you think God placed them there? Has anything like this happened in your own life?

9. A police officer helps Sydney as a young woman to overcome her challenging life and Sydney becomes a police officer to pay it forward. Is there some challenge in your life that you've come through and used the skills or concepts you've learned to help others?

10. If this officer hadn't helped Sydney, what might have happened to her and Nikki? Can you see how important it is to help those in need?

11. Do you really believe God works all things for good, or are there things in your life that you struggle to see good come from?

12. Trust, once broken, is so hard to reclaim. Have you ever been in a relationship where someone has done something to lose your trust? Did they ever regain it, and if so, how? If you are experiencing this problem right now, how can your faith help you through it?

LARGER-PRINT BOOKS!

GET 2 FREE
LARGER-PRINT NOVELS
PLUS 2 FREE
MYSTERY GIFTS

Love Inspired
SUSPENSE
RIVETING INSPIRATIONAL ROMANCE

Larger-print novels are now available...

LARGER-PRINT BOOKS!

GET 2 FREE
LARGER-PRINT NOVELS
PLUS 2 FREE
MYSTERY GIFTS

Larger-print novels are now available...

YES! Please send me 2 FREE LARGER-PRINT Love Inspired® novels and my 2 FREE mystery gifts (gifts are worth about $10). After receiving them, if I don't wish to receive any more books, I can return the shipping statement marked "cancel". If I don't cancel, I will receive 6 brand-new novels every month and be billed just $4.74 per book in the U.S. or $5.24 per book in Canada. That's a saving of at least 24% off the cover price. It's quite a bargain! Shipping and handling is just 50¢ per book in the U.S. and 75¢ per book in Canada.* I understand that accepting the 2 free books and gifts places me under no obligation to buy anything. I can always return a shipment and cancel at any time. Even if I never buy another book, the two free books and gifts are mine to keep forever.

122/322 IDN FC79

Name	(PLEASE PRINT)	
Address		Apt. #
City	State/Prov.	Zip/Postal Code

Signature (if under 18, a parent or guardian must sign)

Mail to the **Reader Service:**
IN U.S.A.: P.O. Box 1867, Buffalo, NY 14240-1867
IN CANADA: P.O. Box 609, Fort Erie, Ontario L2A 5X3

Not valid to current subscribers to Love Inspired Larger-Print books.

Are you a current subscriber to Love Inspired books
and want to receive the larger-print edition?
Call 1-800-873-8635 or visit www.ReaderService.com.

* Terms and prices subject to change without notice. Prices do not include applicable taxes. Sales tax applicable in N.Y. Canadian residents will be charged applicable taxes. Offer not valid in Quebec. This offer is limited to one order per household. All orders subject to credit approval. Credit or debit balances in a customer's account(s) may be offset by any other outstanding balance owed by or to the customer. Please allow 4 to 6 weeks for delivery. Offer available while quantities last.

Your Privacy—The Reader Service is committed to protecting your privacy. Our Privacy Policy is available online at www.ReaderService.com or upon request from the Reader Service.

We make a portion of our mailing list available to reputable third parties that offer products we believe may interest you. If you prefer that we not exchange your name with third parties, or if you wish to clarify or modify your communication preferences, please visit us at www.ReaderService.com/consumerchoice or write to us at Reader Service Preference Service, P.O. Box 9062, Buffalo, NY 14269. Include your complete name and address.

LILP11